Rajinder Singh Bedi was born in Lahore in 1915. After a brief clerical career in the Postal Department he joined All India Radio and was appointed Station Director of Jammu Radio Station in 1948. He resigned from government service soon after and ventured into the film world of Bombay as writer and producer. Notable among the films produced by him was *Garam Coat*. He also wrote the script for the two President Award winners: *Mirza Ghalib* and *Anuradha*.

Rajinder Singh Bedi began by writing English poetry but then moved on to write in Punjabi and then in Urdu. His first collection of short stories was *Dana O Daam*, followed three years later by *Grehan* and *Haath Hamare Kalam Hue*. He also wrote several plays and novels. The Urdu novel *Ek Chadar Maili Si* was awarded the Sahitya Kala Akademi Award in 1965.

Rajinder Singh Bedi died in 1984.

Khushwant Singh is India's best-known journalist and has also had an extremely successful career as a writer. Among the works he has published are a classic two-volume history of the Sikhs, several novels (the best-known of which are *Delhi* and *Train to Pakistan*, which won the Grove Press award for the best work of fiction in 1954), a number of non-fiction books on Delhi, nature and current affairs. An anthology of his best-known writings, *Not A Nice Man To Know: The Best of Khushwant Singh* was published by Penguin India in January 1993.

He has published several translations including *Iqbal's Dialogue with Allah, Umrao Jan Ada—Courtesan of Lucknow, Land of the Five Rivers* and Sheikh Abdullah's autobiography, *Flames of the Chinar*.

Rajinder Singh Bedi

I Take This Woman

Translated from the Urdu by Khushwant Singh

PENGUIN BOOKS

Penguin Books India (P) Ltd., 210, Chiranjiv Tower, 43, Nehru Place, New Delhi 110 019, India
Penguin Books Ltd., 27 Wrights Lane, London W8 5TZ, UK
Penguin Books USA Inc., 375 Hudson Street, New York, New York 10014, USA
Penguin Books Australia Ltd., Ringwood, Victoria, Australia
Penguin Books Canada Ltd., 10 Alcorn Avenue, Suite 300, Toronto, Ontario M4V 3B2, Canada
Penguin Books (NZ) Ltd., 182-190 Wairau Road, Auckland 10, New Zealand

First published as *Ek Chadar Maili Si* by Maktaba Jamia 1962
This translation published by Penguin Books India (P) Ltd. 1994

Copyright © Khushwant Singh 1994

All rights reserved

10 9 8 7 6 5 4 3 2

Typeset in New Baskerville by Digital Technologies and Printing Solutions, New Delhi

This book is sold subject to the condition that it shall not, by way of trade or otherwise, be lent, resold, hired out, or otherwise circulated without the publisher's prior written consent in any form of binding or cover other than that in which it is published and without a similar condition including this condition being imposed on the subsequent purchaser and without limiting the rights under copyright reserved above, no part of this publication may be reproduced, stored in or introduced into a retrieval system, or transmitted in any form or by any means (electronic, mechanical, photocopying, recording or otherwise), without the prior written permission of both the copyright owner and the above-mentioned publisher of this book.

Our blood is in the red of the dawn and of the dusk...

— Majrooh

Contents

One 3
Two 17
Three 41
Four 59
Five 83
Six 109

Contents

One 3
Two 17
Three 14
Four 39
Five 83
Six 109

One

The sun was a deeper red; the heavens were a darker crimson as if spattered with the blood of innocents: the stream of blood ran from the sky down into Tiloka's courtyard, tinting the green of the *bakain* with hues of purple. Beside the tumble-down mud wall where garbage was thrown sat Dabboo. He raised his head to the heavens and set up a piteous howl.

That afternoon the sweepers of the Rural District Council had come and strewn pellets of poisoned meat in the lanes. At the time Dabboo was asleep in the cool fragrance of the sand beneath the pitcher rack. The clay-scented shade had saved Dabboo from the fate which befell many of his kin—particularly his favourite, Bori. After many hours of peaceful slumber, he had risen, stretched his limbs and yawned. By that time Bori's eyes had turned to marbles. Dabboo scampered out of the courtyard and found her carcass, as stiff as a log. He sniffed at her posterior and quietly turned back homewards.

Tiloka's wife, Rano, and her neighbour, Channo, watched Dabboo come and go. Channo put a finger on the gold pin in her nose and breathed a long sigh. 'Disgusting, isn't it!' she exclaimed. 'The males of the species are all the same; they deserve to be strung by the same rope.'

Rano's eyelids quivered like washing fluttering on a line. She brushed away her tears with the back of her hand and smiled, 'Channo, I hope your Dabboo is not like this one.' She was overcome with her audacity. Channo replied with a masculine oath, ran back into her house and busied herself with her household chores. By the time she had finished her work she had all but forgotten the tragic scene of the afternoon. But when she came out to throw the refuse on the garbage heap, Dabboo was there to remind her of his fate. Channo picked up her broom and shooed away the wailing Dabboo. 'Begone, you miserable dog! Why do you howl in my courtyard? If you have to wail, go and wail in the Chaudhry's courtyard across the lane. The mob is there—and the money as well.'

Rano hated Chaudhry Meharban Das. She hated him because it was Meharban Das who had initiated her husband into his evil ways. Village women are like that: they will overlook every fault of their husbands by pinning them on to other men. When Rano heard about Tiloka's doings from anyone, although she would be all burnt up inside her, she would keep a straight face and say nothing. But when Tiloka returned home she would give him a proper tongue-lashing. She would claw his face. She would bite him. She would keep going at him till he beat her. Then she would become quiet and say with philosophic resignation: 'Just as well he spills his passion elsewhere; otherwise I would have to cope with all of it.'

*

It was only from gossip in the village that Rano came to know of the 'manly' qualities of her husband. It created a perverse desire in her to claim his affections exclusively for herself. She went to the holy man who had set himself up beneath the leafless peepul tree. He was said to have undergone arduous penance and thus gathered great merit. It was said that he wore a steel bracket about his loins and never deigned to look at women. This was all the more credible as he was surrounded by hordes of women at all hours of the day and night. Some came to ask for sons; others for medicine for protection against miscarriage. Most came for charms to keep their husbands in their power.

Everyone talked of the case of Pooran Dei, the Brahmin's wife. The charm that the holy one gave her not only filled her womb but also made her husband, Gian Chand, dote on her like one possessed. Rano had got some powder from the holy one. She was only awaiting the chance to administer it to Tiloka when he asked for milk. She looked forward to the night when he would take the milk with the magic powder and his passions would be roused. Then she would not let him touch her—or only after he begged her for the favour by touching her feet and rubbing his nose in the dust. But many weeks had passed without Tiloka asking for milk. Instead, he quenched his thirst with the bottle of orange liquor he got from Chaudhry Meharban Das.

Rano could forgive most things, but not drink. To her the bottle of liquor was like a second wife in the house. The stench of alcohol! Holy Mother, it made her sick to think of it! And once drunk, the devil took possession of you, body and soul. It was absolute damnation.

During the day Tiloka plied his tonga. So did many others like Nawab, Ismail and Gurdas. But in the evening it would only be Tiloka at the Naseebanwala tonga-stand looking for a female passenger for Chaudhry Meharban Das' 'rest house', with its promise of dainty dishes consumed in a cosy bed. To be sure, Tiloka took all this trouble for Chaudhry Meharban Das. But everyone blamed him. And all he got for his pains was half a chop of meat and a bottle of distilled orange liquor.

Kotla was a place of pilgrimage. On one side of the Chaudhry's courtyard was the shrine of the Goddess. It was said that she had rested there for a breather while fleeing from her lusty Bhairon; she had then gone on to find shelter in the hills of Sialkot and Jammu. If one looked up to the north-west one could still see a camel-hump formation in the range of hills near Dumel. This was the famous peak named after the Goddess—Vaishno Devi.

The passenger that Tiloka brought to the Chaudhry that evening was barely thirteen years old. When Bhairon had lusted after Vaishno Devi she had decapitated him with her trident. The poor thirteen-year-old innocent had only a pair of hands as soft as rose petals to defend herself against the Chaudhry's amours. She put them together in a prayer to be left alone, but that was of little avail. Her skin was as soft as that of a water-melon—and as easy to pierce with the knife of lust that Meharban Das used. No wonder then that the sun had turned a fiery red! And no wonder that the God Surya had in his rage whipped his horses to a mad gallop, driven his chariot across the village well and disappeared behind the cotton fields! He had left his angry glow in the heavens. The pale moon, barely two days old, shimmered in a paler sky.

Next door to the temple was the contractor's house. He was having repairs done to his roof. The shades of twilight had spread over his walls. The red of the bricks could not be seen but the lime plaster showed like grinning teeth. The breeze whistled through the casuarina, jamun and neem trees that lined the watercourse. Beside the pond, the stunted peepul which had sheltered Baba Hari Das clapped its few leaves as if beating time to music. Tiloka was driving through the only bazaar of the village, past its only flour and grain shop, when he chanced to see a lone woman. It was the Arain woman, Jhelum, buying wheat. Tiloka shouted to her: 'What about it, Jhelum, old girl?'

It is a well-known saying that a poor man's wife is everyone's sister-in-law. Jhelum was used to villagers making passes at her. She did not bother to look round. She continued filling her sack as she replied, 'If your mother's willing, why not go to her?'

Tiloka laughed and continued on his way.

Tiloka's twin sons were playing ludo on a charcoal-drawn pattern under the neem tree. One boy scored a kill; the other objected. A veritable bedlam was let loose. The boys cursed in the language used by their elders, and pulled each other's hair. As soon as they heard their father's footsteps, they separated, grabbed their primers and quickly sat down beside the oil lamp. Tiloka called to them. The elder of the two replied by reciting loudly from his book: 'Look, the owl hoots in yonder tree.' Tiloka knew his sons. 'You bastards! Don't try these tricks on me!' he yelled. The younger one took up the recitation: 'We should never use bad language. We should never use bad language.' Tiloka realized the import of these words of wisdom and held his tongue.

Besides the twins, Bantey and Santey, there were two more. Their older child, the first-born, the parents had for the sake of simplicity and posterity named Waddi, the elder. She lent her mother a helping hand in the home; and when the chores were done, she looked after the youngest, the one-year-old, Chummoo.

My brother's come back from play, he's hungry
I'll roll and bake him a maund to eat.

Even when she played pat-ball with other girls of the neighbourhood, Waddi's songs were of her little brother:

We've come on to our rooftop
I've a brother tall as a bamboo
My brother's wife is slender as the cypress
My brother's wife wears gold in her nose.

In this way Waddi brought people and objects familiar to her into her verses: sugar-cane, her little brother, her sister-in-law and her nose-ring, the leafless peepul tree, the husband's elder brother (her horizon had expanded to her future husband's elder brother—but she had only a vague and hazy notion of who or what he or it might be).

There was another member of the household who was rapidly catching on to the facts of life. This was Tiloka's younger brother, Mangal. Mangal was an incorrigible idler, a good-for-nothing drone, quarrelling and getting into brawls, forever adjusting his *tehmat* around his waist. And Rano, who really liked him, always feigned ill-temper when she chided him: 'Patience, you big oaf! Who do you think I've cooked all this stuff for except you?'

Mangal was barely six years old when Tiloka had acquired Rano. Rano's parents were destitute (perhaps that was why they had named their daughter dressed in tatters, Rani, or Rano). As Rano grew to womanhood her needs became a problem. So they sold her to Tiloka and simply disappeared from their village. This caused Rano great distress. However poor a parents' home, it is something every girl cherishes. For Rano, the past had simply ceased to exit. There come moments in a woman's married life when she seeks the security of her parental home ... and if she has no home to go back to she feels she has nothing to look forward to either.

When Rano came to Kotla, she found new parents and a brother: her mother-in-law, Jindan, became a new mother, and her father-in-law, Hazoor Singh, a new father. But her husband's youngest brother, Mangal, was a mere baby. Once when she was giving the breast to Waddi and Mangal had wanted to feed, Rano had raised her shirt and offered him her other breast. The boy had run away ... but Rano thereafter had looked upon Mangal as her own son.

Mangal also looked upon Rano both as his brother's wife and as his mother. For what other reason would he have addressed his real mother as Aunty? And Rano treated him as she treated her other children. She boxed his ears when he was stubborn and slapped his face when he was errant. But as the years went by things began to change. Rano had other children to look after; Mangal took on the airs of an adolescent; Tiloka took to the bottle; old Jindan became the traditional nagging mother-in-law. The real cause of the trouble was their poverty. As Tiloka began to stay at home two or three days in the week, they had less money coming in. Then old Hazoor Singh got cataracts in his eyes. He would sit on his charpoy trying to see with his ears and hear with his frosted eyes. His eyelids fluttered like those of the pigeons bathing in the village pond.

*

One evening, Tiloka took a tomato from the pocket of his long shirt and ordered his wife: 'Here, Rano, slice it up with an onion.'

Rano was busy cooking vegetables. She put the ladle on the pot and stood up. 'You've brought your other wife into the house?' she demanded.

Tiloka faltered in his speech. 'I don't do it very often, do I, Rano?'

'Often or not, I am not going to let you drink here,' replied Rano tartly. 'Where is the bottle? I'd like to see what she has that I have not.'

Tiloka did not want a scene. But Rano was obviously spoiling for a fight. He ground his teeth and hissed as angrily as he could hoping in vain to silence her: 'Bitch! Whore! I try to hold my horses but you go full gallop with your foul tongue.'

'Sure!' spat out Rano. 'I suppose no one else but you is entitled to give rein to the tongue! I am going to settle this business once for all. Either I stay in this house or your bottle does.'

Rano ran inside to look for the 'second wife'. Tiloka ran after her. He caught Rano by her hair and flung her to the ground. The oil lamp flickered . . . it almost went out but came up again . . . the starling on the neem tree flew away in alarm . . . Dabboo stood up and, being unable to comprehend the goings on, began to bark . . . Waddi cried out in alarm, 'Bapoo!' . . . the little ones were terrified and tried to hide themselves in the dark: one ran out of the house, the other shook with fright and began to wail—not 'Ma . . . Ma . . .' but just 'Aaa . . . aa . . . .' Hazoor Singh stumbled from his charpoy and pleaded as he swore, '*Oi*, you son of fornication! *Oi*, you evil, shameless, mannerless brute!' He stumbled and fell on to the oven and scorched himself on the embers.

Rano put up a good fight. She dug her teeth into Tiloka's hands. This enraged Tiloka all the more and he hammered Rano's head against the wall. And he used language that he had never used even to an animal. 'Help! Murder!' screamed Waddi. 'He's killing my mother!' By the time her grandmother came in, Waddi had wet her salwar. Granny saw the fight and exclaimed: 'I knew one day things would come to a head; one day this moon of evil would shine in our courtyard. What did we do to have this vagrant seed take root in our home?'

'Why do you stick your nose into this affair?' snapped Mangal at his mother. He did not think it was right to interfere in a quarrel between husband and wife and was doing his utmost to keep out of the brawl.

'Why shouldn't I stick my nose in wherever I like?' shrieked the old woman. 'He earns, he drinks.

He does not go begging to the door of that pimp who's gone to hell himself and left this sluttish daughter with us!'

His mother's words made Tiloka more violent. He tore off Rano's clothes till she had nothing left on her. And he yelled as loud as he could, 'Get out! Get out of my house at once!'

Rano was out of breath. She started to moan. 'I won't live here. I'll leave, myself.'

A line of faces appeared over the mud wall. A crowd collected on the neighbouring rooftops. 'He's killed her! The devil, he's murdered her! *Hai*, this ogre!' they cried from all sides. But not one had the courage to come down to help Rano. Jhelum Arain heard the racket and came across the roof. With her were her daughters, the Brahmin woman, Pooran Dei, Nawab's wife Ayesha, Channo and Sarupa. They all came up, but only Channo dared to cry for help: 'Help! Someone separate them!'

'Keep out of this!' shouted Rano from where she lay, hardly able to breathe. 'Go away! Haven't you ever had a thrashing? Let what is destined be fulfilled. Today the Devi is going to have her great offering. I am to be sacrificed by this man. I'll go to heaven. My children will wail for me today,' cried Rano, trying to send away the women and at the same time beckoning them.

Mangal had been restraining himself for all he was worth. Suddenly it became too much for him. He yelled full-mouthed abuse at his mother and sprang at his brother. He grabbed his brother's hand as it was raised to strike. 'Let me see you bring this hand down!' he roared. 'I'll show you the dung you are made of . . . you who show off your strength on a weak woman! Try and move your hand, if you are the son of your father! You just try!'

Tiloka did his best to wrench his arm free of Mangal's iron grip. It was to no avail. He turned to abuse him. He saw the murderous look in his younger brother's eyes and thought better of it. Mangal took full advantage of his triumph. He kicked the bottle of liquor. It crashed on the floor and the liquor spilled in the courtyard. The women drew their veils across their nostrils to save themselves from the stench. Mangal let go of his brother's hand after he had thoroughly humiliated him. Tiloka went indoors mumbling angrily to himself. His foul words had lost their sting; they seemed to roll off his tongue like lines from a book.

Rano also went indoors and began to pack her things in her little steel trunk. She was going away. Where could she go to? 'O God, do not burden even an enemy with the curse of a daughter! She is hardly grown up when her parents throw her out to live among strangers; and if the parents-in-law don't like her, they kick her back to her parents' home. She's like a ball made of cast-off rags. Only when she becomes heavy with her own tears is she incapable of being bounced to and fro.'

Rano did not have much to pack. In a few moments all her belongings were in the steel trunk. She came out of the room carrying her load. She resumed her wailing louder than before. It was meant to bring tears to the eyes of the other women.

'Here, keep your home; may it ever be prosperous! I was the only unwanted outsider . . . I will relieve you of my burden.' She turned towards the room into which Tiloka had gone. 'Get yourself another woman who'll be your slave . . . who will love to have her bones broken . . . .' Her eyes fell on her children: in her rage and sorrow she had forgotten their existence. 'Children!' she exclaimed, 'I'll say I never had; I'll say they died at birth.'

Waddi caught the hem of her mother's dupatta and cried, 'Ma!'

Rano snatched her dupatta from her daughter's grip. 'Get away with you, you accursed one! When your time comes, you too will have to put up with this kind of treatment!'

*

Rano strode out into the great, big, limitless world. It was pitch dark. She could see nothing but the stars in the sky. Each of these stars was as large as her world, some even larger. And there they were, twinkling before her eyes. A small cloud floated across and cut the crescent moon in two . . . .

Mangal followed Rano. He took her by the arm and asked, 'Sister-in-law, where are you going?' Then Mangal turned to his mother and pleaded, 'Aunty, why don't you stop her?'

Jindan brushed her hands against the hem of her shirt and exclaimed, 'Where can the wretch go! She has nothing to fall back on; no one to go to.'

Hazoor Singh shouted from where he was, 'Daughter... Rano...' and then began to walk towards her. When he got closer, he raised his shirt and showed her the burns on his back. 'Daughter, see what I have suffered.'

Rano broke down. She covered her face with her dupatta; she could utter only one word, 'Bapu!' By then Tiloka's temper had cooled. He stood like an unwanted orphan in a corner of his courtyard. His threats lacked conviction. 'Go! Let me see where you can go.'

'I'll go where I like! What's that to do with you?' retorted Rano, wailing louder. 'I'll take a job somewhere; I'll earn enough to fill my belly. I am not going to be a burden on any one for the sake of a couple of chapattis. If there is no other place for me in the village, I will go to the temple.'

'The temple!' roared Tiloka, somewhat startled. He stepped before her, snatched the trunk out of Rano's hand and said, 'Follow me.... Then you go to hell!'

To go forward into the wide world or turn back?... Rano's self-esteem required her to protest some more. And protest she did. But her recriminations like her husband's abuse had lost their punch. All she wanted was an excuse to save face as well as be able to come back. And what was the point of leaving? The bottle of liquor had been smashed.

Two

Rano plastered a poultice on Hazoor Singh's burns and came back to her room. Tiloka lay on his back with his legs outstretched: he was lost in his thoughts. The little one began to cry. Rano gave him her breast; he went back to sleep. The turmoil of the afternoon had ceased to agitate Tiloka's mind; instead thoughts of the 'pilgrim' of the earlier evening went round and round in his head. In the dark he had visualized himself as Chaudhry Meharban Das and Rano as the 'pilgrim' woman. He stretched out his hand towards Rano. Rano brushed it away. 'You are like a child; you'll never grow up,' said Tiloka trying to make up. 'You behave exactly like a twelve-year-old. You have tantrums like a little girl.'

He began to plead with her. He was the type who lost all his pride as soon as the lamps were extinguished and it became dark.

He got up. From the alcove he fetched the picture of Shiva with the Ganga cascading out of his top-knot. Parvati was seated beside Shiva. He placed the picture beside Rano and pleaded with her in the name of Shiva to come and be reasonable. He told her of Parvati's undying love for her husband. Rano did not budge. Tiloka brought another picture. This one was of Radha and Krishna. He took it out of its frame . . . . Like one possessed he went on taking pictures out of their frames . . . . Soon the place was littered with wood and glass.

When Rano awoke in the morning her limbs were sore. She found it difficult to get up from her charpoy. The household work needed doing. No one had had anything to eat the previous evening; so she was expected to give them their morning meal earlier than usual. She had to prepare meal for the horse, and take out the harness and trappings. And there was Tiloka sleeping like one dead, with his eyes half open and his mouth gaping like a cavern. Rano went to the niche and picked up the oil lamp. She stood beside Tiloka's charpoy and saw him under the light—like one who returns to see the serpent he has killed.

By the time Tiloka woke, Rano had got through a great deal of work. Not a trace of what had happened the evening before showed on her face. It was the same with Tiloka. As was his wont, he wrinkled an angry eyebrow when Rano gave him the harness—as if he had never pulled his own ears or drawn lines with his nose in gestures of repentance or craved forgiveness a few hours earlier. The sun's rays had rekindled his masculine pride. As he took the harness, the bells tinkled and the feathered plume fluttered in the breeze. 'Don't you be under any illusion that I am scared of you,' he said.

'I didn't say anything,' replied Rano.

Tiloka could not let that pass. 'Only the impotent are scared of their women. I am going to get another bottle of orange liquor today. I'd like to see you try and stop me.'

Rano remained silent. But in her mind she thought of many things she might do. 'If he brings liquor into the house again, I will swallow a mouthful of arsenic . . . or stab my belly with the antlers of a stag . . . or take some of the dog poison they gave to kill the bitch, Bori. Like that dog Dabboo, this wretch will only sniff at my corpse and turn away. He may shed a tear or two—if not for me, at least for his motherless children . . . . Who the hell cares whether I am alive or dead! Only parents miss their children . . . . Where are my parents? No one to go back to; nothing to look forward to. No, I must not die, it will only please my mother-in-law, who will undoubtedly say, "Good riddance!" '

While she was lost in thought, Mangal happened to pass by. The brothers glowered at each other. 'So you've got ready, you drone!' exclaimed Tiloka—and then turned away like a dog with its tail between its legs. Mangal made no retort, but quietly went out of the house.

Waddi saw her parents talking to each other and slipped out into the courtyard; she busied herself getting her brothers ready for school. In the next room, Hazoor Singh, who had spent most of the night groaning, was fast asleep. Next to him Jindan was mumbling her morning prayer.

A little later an ekka loaded with passengers stopped by the door and Rano, as usual, handed Tiloka a bundle of four thick chapattis and some greasy, spicy vegetable curry. Rano glanced at the passengers. Among them was a girl barely thirteen years old in a semi-conscious state. Chaudhry Meharban Das' servants seemed to be in charge and were taking her back to the city. 'Who is she? What's the matter with her?' enquired Rano.

'Epileptic,' replied Tiloka as he tightened the harness.

'Epilepsy?' demanded Rano in a tone of disbelief, with her finger on her nose.

'Of course!' repeated Tiloka. 'The sort of epileptic fit most women get; you had an attack last night. The only way to treat it is to give the shoe,' he nodded towards the open door and continued, 'or the whip. I'll try it out on you tonight. I've just had a new thong put on it.'

Rano felt weak in the knees. The first thing she did as soon as Tiloka was out of sight was to take the whip from the shelf and bury it deep in a sack of wheat in the storeroom.

*

That afternoon a mob came running across the village common: amongst them were two ekka drivers, Nawab and Ismail. They came up to Pooran Dei's husband, Gyan Chand, and the miller, Diwana, and said, 'Pandit, have you heard . . . ?' They whispered something in Pandit's ear. Then they all went into a huddle. Meanwhile, Jhelum's son-in-law, Morad Baksh, was seen coming from his shop. He had a pair of scales in one hand and a two-seer weight in the other. He was standing in the way of the peasant, Shahi. He said something to the peasant. They joined the others and began looking at Tiloka's house. Rano stood in her courtyard, gaping at the crowd staring at her.

Channo, who had come to see her the previous evening, shook her by the shoulder. 'Tell me, what's happened?'

Rano nodded towards the men. 'I don't know what's come over these men? They are staring at me,' she replied somewhat bewildered.

'You know why, don't you?' asked Channo.

'No. Why?'

'Last night's thrashing must have unhinged you.'

'Slut! Devourer of your husband!' swore Rano as she grabbed Channo by her pigtail. The two dug each other in the ribs, tickled each other under the armpits and burst into peals of laughter.

The women turned to see the crowd. And what Rano saw gave her immense pleasure. She saw Chaudhry Meharban Das and his brother Ghanisham Das in handcuffs being led through the bazaar. With them was a lad of about eighteen, whose clothes were stained with blood. Even his face and body were spattered with red. The boy was in a daze and had to be helped by the police sergeant and the village headman. Meharban Das looked blacker than before; his ear-rings glistened brighter. Ghanisham Das had injuries on his forehead; his turban hung loosely about his neck as if he had had no time to wind it, or as if it had been knocked about in a brawl.

'Thank God!' exclaimed Rano. 'Channo, I will celebrate this by giving everyone sugar-candy. They've been molesting other people's daughters; now they will be the sons-in-law of the government.' Rano clapped her hands and began to dance. 'I am going to dance; I am going to dance the *gidda*.' She looked towards the spire of the temple, and joined her palms in prayer: 'Goddess Devi, most Holy Mother, I thank you ... you heard my prayer .... The day has been blessed!'

She saw Tiloka's ekka coming along, driven not by Tiloka but by Gurdas.

'*Hai*!' exclaimed Rano in alarm. She could see a recumbent figure in the ekka. Was it that girl in an epileptic fit? The passengers lent a helping hand to get the 'girl' off the ekka. The corpse was unloaded and its face uncovered. Rano let out a piercing yell. 'No, no!' she cried as she ran indoors. Channo beat her forehead and breast as she ran back to her home.

Tiloka was dead—murdered. The young girl's brother had found him near the well. He had fastened his teeth in Tiloka's gullet and had not let go till every drop of Tiloka's blood had been drained out of his body.

When the villagers caught him, the lad was in a state of religious frenzy. His eyes were riveted on the steeple of the temple. He flung his arms in the air screaming, 'Goddess divine, you have been avenged! I did it for you!' While the villagers beat him and dragged him along, he sang a hymn to the Devi.

In the durbar of the Mother Goddess,
The Queen Celestial,
The lamps are lit.
In the court of the Queen Mother
Eternal lamps are lit.

Indeed, the torches had been lit in the court of the Queen Mother and the glitter of their flames was reflected in the boy's large, demoniac eyes. His skin would turn a pale yellow; and then turn an angry red. He stumbled through the crowd till he reached the temple. Then he went leaping, dancing and yelling:

O, Mother divine!
Seven fair sisters are with you;
With two coral flowers in your hair.
In my Queen Mother's durbar,
Is lit the eternal light.

The boy had squeezed the blood out of his clothes and smeared it on his hair. It seemed as if the spirit of the Goddess had entered his soul; the spirit of revenge had set his eyes aflame and he looked upon Tiloka as the Devi had looked upon her ravisher, Bhairon. He prostrated himself at the temple door and then stood up straight. The villagers were frightened at the spectacle; some even trembled with fear. They left the boy alone and stood at a distance. If he had wanted, he could have continued roaring, ranting and singing. If he had wanted, he could have got away. But a little later he surrendered himself to the headman. Perhaps this too was an act of lunacy.

The news spread to the neighbouring villages. There was a great hubbub in Kotla. Unseasonal clouds dimmed the sun; twilight came before its time. The steeple of Vaishno Devi's temple seemed to peer into Tiloka's yard. The leaves of the neem withered before their time. Instead of barking as he used to, Dabboo put his tail between his legs and slunk away behind the pile of fodder.

The light came back into Hazoor Singh's eyes—only to see his son's corpse. Jindan saw and lost consciousness—she was spared the wailing and screaming of the children. Rano ran out of the house, ran back, and then out again. She could not make anything of the incident. She had a mad impulse to wear her best clothes and adorn herself with the trinkets she possessed. Before she could do this, Channo caught hold of her and smashed her glass bangles against the wall. Pooran Dei brought a palmful of dust from the street and poured it over Rano's head.

But Rano could not understand what had happened. Once again she went indoors and began to dig in the sack of grain like a bitch digs up the earth with its claws before she has her litter.... Rano pulled out the whip with the new thongs. In her blind rage she flaunted it before Tiloka's corpse and then, under the eyes of the crowd, broke it into two: 'See what I have done to your whip! You big braggart! You were going to break it on my back, weren't you?'

People looked askance: was Rano out of her mind? Yes, Rano was both out of her mind, and yet not quite mad. Waddi put her head against the wall and wailed loudly. Rano went up to her and smacked her with both her hands.

'Crops are killed by hail, children are killed by the pox—everyone dies except you. Nothing happens to you.'

A woman ran up and rescued Waddi. 'What's the poor girl done?' she demanded.

'It's all her fault,' screamed Rano. 'Why was she born in the house of a father who was to die before arranging his daughter's marriage?' And suddenly it flashed across Rano's mind as she stood on the threshold. 'Silly woman,' she said to herself, 'if you do not cry now, you'll become the laughing-stock of the world.' But tears would not come to her eyes. Her own children appeared to be strangers; her house an alien place.

She went in. Perhaps she could crush an onion in front of her eyes. In the end she did not have to look for anything like that: right in front of her was the saucer with the tomato which Tiloka had wanted to eat with his bottle of orange liquor. Then the dam burst. She began to cry; she began to wail; she smacked her forehead with both her hands. The women of the village joined in her wailing and tried to stop her at the same time. Rano's screams rose to the heavens; she bashed her head against the walls; tears flowed down her cheeks and she drooled from her mouth. 'Rano my child—you had no parents and now you have no husband either,' she lamented.

'Whore! You are too old to earn a living in the bazaar; you aren't fit even to be a tart.'

*

Chaudhry Meharban Das, his brother, Ghanisham Das and Baba Hari Das were sentenced to seven years' rigorous imprisonment each. The brother of the girl who had been raped (and who had thereupon murdered Tiloka) was given the same term in gaol, because the counsel for defence was able to prove grave and sudden provocation and so have the young man's crime reduced from murder to manslaughter. Why the heavy sentence on Baba Hari Das? Because his 'chastity belt' had proved to be made not of steel, as was reputed, but of brocade.

The sentence on Baba Hari Das came as a great surprise to the women of Kotla. They looked at each other for an explanation. The one to be pilloried was the Brahmin woman, Pooran Dei, who was the biggest windbag in the village. She was caught out, because her spontaneous reaction on hearing the news was, 'Of course.' At the same time her eyes filled with tears.... People said that although the hill of Vaishno Devi was fifty miles away, the Goddess kept her protective eye on Kotla; people of charity and faith, people who fed pigeons at the village pond and other righteous ones, would be preserved from harm; no sin could be committed in Kotla. And if it was, it would meet with the same condign punishment as was meted out to Bhairon when he tried to ravish Vaishno Devi.

To meet the expenses of the case, the Chaudhrys had to sell all their property, their homes and even their kitchen utensils. The Panchayat took over the custody and management of the village temple. Tiloka's murder had taught the villagers a lesson. Thereafter no man dared to raise his eyes at a woman. When village girls came out in their finery, the men just gaped at their figures and lauded their movements with silent eyes; often they did not have the courage even to gape.

Hazoor Singh got water in his bones. He sat on his charpoy listening to old Jindan's gossip. Jindan recalled the times when she was the grand mistress of Hazoor Singh's home and affections. He had taken her to big cities; they had visited zoos and aviaries. And now the same Hazoor Singh could do nothing more than sit on his charpoy and recite the melancholic hymns of the Ninth Guru on the transitoriness of life. These hymns infused Hazoor Singh with a strange sense of courage and peace.

As for Jindan, she could not stop grumbling and grousing. The mere sight of Rano would make her hackles rise and she would shower her with bucketfuls of abuse: 'Whore! Witch! Ogress! You ate my son. And now you have your mouth wide open to swallow the rest of us. Get out! Go whichever way your fancy takes you. There's no place for you in this home.'

Rano would not have stayed a moment longer than she had to. But her children entangled her heart as if she were a fly in a spider's web. The more Jindan tried to push her out, the more Rano begged to be allowed to stay. Finding herself so utterly unwanted began to tell on her health. But while Rano was withering away, the sap of life made her daughter, Waddi, blossom. Waddi was like a jungle flower which bursts into full bloom with wild abandon. She became carefree and happy. She was always singing and dancing. On moonlit nights she went out to play with the boys of the village.

Whenever Waddi was late Rano gave her a sound thrashing—almost as if she were threshing rice stalks. It made no difference to Waddi. To avoid her daughter's attracting attention, Rano kept her in rags (partly because they were poor and partly by plan). She never combed Waddi's hair, but let it scatter untidily over her face so that no one would cast an evil eye on the girl. But Waddi was fair and comely and, as Pooran Dei often said, the girl looked as if she had English blood in her veins. If anyone cast an amorous glance at Waddi, Rano would be on the war-path. And when the crisis was over she would recite:

O God, let her not be very fair.
The entire village has become my enemy.

The more Rano tried to keep her daughter in hiding or dressed in old rags, the more Waddi's burgeoning youth burst through. She had the wide-eyed innocence of a child who rushes up to the window whenever the sound of martial music falls on its ears. Rano despaired of Waddi's simple and unsuspicious nature; she feared that, deprived as she was of a father's protection, Waddi would come to a bad end; the day one of their enemies took a fancy to the girl, she would be a goner. The anxiety for the child's future weighed on Rano. She began to lose weight. Then she began to have fainting fits.

According to Rano's way of looking at things, Waddi was getting closer and closer to the day of destiny. From the month of December, Rano had kept count of Waddi's periods. If the girl was a day or two overdue, Rano would badger her with all kinds of improper questions: 'Where were you in the afternoon? Where did you go after you left Eeshro? Who were the people in the temple? Why did you ask the priest for a mantra? You know what such mantras will do to you? Have you already forgotten about Baba Hari Das?' And so on.

Rano began to collect things for her daughter's dowry. She began to think of finding a young man who would take her away as soon as possible. But there was not a cowrie to give to the girl. Then Rano thought of her own past. She had been given away to Tiloka on the promise that he would feed and clothe her—nothing more. Fate was more unkind to her daughter, who was not even provided with food and clothing.

Rano's main worry were the boys of the village. The bastards would go to the cinema at Daska and forget the difference between their mothers and sisters and other women. If she could find one decent lad amongst them, someone who could respect the women of Kotla, she might consider him as a husband for Waddi. That would be the end of all her worries. But the village lads were a bunch of hooligans. They were always raiding Mehr Karam Deen's citrus grove. They would eat some of the fruit, waste most of it, despoil the trees, and run away. There was no one to tame this wild lot.

What had destiny in store for Waddi? Wairowal or Daska? Budha Guraya or Jamanki? Or some place a long way away—some place like Lahore or Peshawar? Rano sat and day-dreamed. She treated the span of time between then and the day her daughter would leave her like a concertina—sometimes stretched to its full length like age itself, sometimes shortened to tomorrow. These day-dreams made her giddy. When she and Waddi were embroidering clothes for the dowry, she would start humming:

All girls must be betrothed
All must wed and leave their homes.

What about her own wedding? And her mother- and father-in-law who had now perforce taken the place of her parents? Between her dreaming and her needlework, Rano often forgot that the song she hummed was not of life but of death. And suddenly Rano would feel in better spirits and the desire to go to a real husband would fill her being. When Rano had come to Kotla, Tiloka had not given her much time to think about her equation with her future mother- and father-in-law.

The home of her husband's parents has all kinds of connotations for a girl who comes to it as a proper bride after proper ceremonies and properly veiled: for her there is a ceremonious welcome and anointing with mustard oil; she is subjected to friendly banter and is fussed over by her husband's mother and mollycoddled by his father; for her there are songs and games, the changing of utensils, gifts for raising her veil—which for the bridal night is made of jasmine flowers; for her there is the first night in a room dimly lit by an oil lamp, full of elemental lust and coyness mixed together. This was not the sort of home Tiloka had brought her to; it was not the sort of house girls longed to go to when they were married and looked forward to returning to.

Rano suddenly became aware of her own need for a proper home. Was this concern really for her daughter . . . or for herself? . . she could not decide for a moment. And the song she used to sing was made yet more poignant because of the abuse and nagging of Jindan:

*What use is the body
If it cannot toil?
What use is life
If it's not shared with a friend?*

Then there was that oaf, Mangal, at the Naseebanwala tonga-stand. He had learnt how to put the horse in harness, but had eluded the harness of responsibility. There was less money in the house than ever before. Mangal had been pitchforked into manhood and promptly lost himself in the jungle of desire. Although he had no conception of profit or loss, he understood the basic things of life. Whenever a village wench passed by, the following words escaped his lips:

*O thou sealed bottle of ruby red wine!
The lucky one will uncork thee and drink thy heady nectar.*

Mangal the ekka-driver did not realize that he owed some obligation to the house in which he lived, whose other inmates had been compelled to forgo one meal in the day.

Mangal started a liaison with Salamat, the youngest daughter of the Arain woman, Jhelum. One day the girl made a pass at Mangal: 'Mangal, my lad, how are things?'

Mangal was driving out his ekka. He pulled up the horse and turned round to face Salamat;

Salamat sidled up to him and spoke coquettishly: 'Boy, what about taking us for a ride?'

'Why not? What's the ekka meant for?'

'When?' she demanded, with her eyes half-closed.

'Whenever you say.'

Salamat looked around to see if anyone was about, then she whispered, 'What about tonight?'

'Not at night,' replied Mangal. 'I can't take the ekka out in the dark.'

He whipped up his horse and was away. When he had gone some distance on the road to Satraha, he realized the import of Salamat's words. He wanted to turn back to the village; but by then he had passengers in his ekka. There were still many hours to sunset. He applied the whip with greater zest. 'Gee up, sweetie! On to the city!'

*

When Mangal returned home in the evening, the sight of his impoverished and hungry household killed his appetite for romance. No one had eaten a morsel since the morning; nothing had been cooked. Waddi had boiled a handful of rice. Rano had not been able to restrain her hunger and had swallowed the rice without adding salt or pepper—without a thought for her old parents-in-law or even her young children. And the mother-in-law was giving Rano a lashing with her tongue.

Rano could have strangled the old woman with

her hands, but a strange fear possessed her and she whimpered helplessly. Mangal saw this and stood silent under the neem tree. He had earned a bare fourteen annas that day. It was hardly enough to buy salt and cooking oil. He could have earned another rupee or more, but the passenger wanted to go in the opposite direction. And Mangal was anxious to return to Kotla and Salamat.

Mangal caught his mother's hand, 'Aunty, why do you keep going for this poor woman? Why do you beat her and kick her about? Where can she go?'

Rano, who had not wept so at her husband's death, broke down and sobbed bitterly: 'Why should I get out? What haven't I done for this family? Haven't I borne a son? Haven't I borne a daughter? What is it that I have not . . . ?

'It's not Rano's fault, it's mine,' said Mangal.

'What have you to do with it?' snapped old Jindan. 'A woman who can't act like a mother to her own children is of no use to anyone.' She turned to Rano and with her palms joined in prayer said in a voice loaded with sarcasm, 'In the name of God and the Great Guru and Goddess Vaishno Devi, relieve us of your presence. Get out! Go and find yourself a man—just any man, blind or one-eyed, who'll take you. But get the hell out of here!'

Rano got up and glowered at her mother-in-law. She did not utter the words, but her eyes seemed to say: 'You are the Great Mother! You should not be the one to spurn me! However inconvenient, you should put up with me; I have no one else in the world I can call mine.' It was this galling sense of insecurity that had made her eat up all the rice. And now she did not know how she could continue living in the house.

The children were grown up; and by the law they were Tiloka's more than hers. Even if her in-laws and the village elders allowed her the custody of the children, where could she take them? She would have to beg and teach her children how to beg. She loved all the four, Waddi, Banta, Santa and Chummoo, equally. They were still dependent on her. If she thought of leaving one, her heart ached with pain. They were neither too young to be taken along, nor old enough to be left on their own. Her mother-in-law never spared her: the slipper when she got up, a kick when she sat down. Rano came to believe that this was ordained for all women after they had lost their husbands. She had no right to live in the house any more; no right to continue living anywhere in the world.

*

One day Channo put her arm around Rano and took her home. She gave her wheat chapattis and spinach. Although famished, poor Rano did not eat her fill lest Channo should not invite her again. Channo drew her stool close to Rano and spoke to her. 'Listen, sister: I am going to say something to you if you promise to pay heed to my words.'

Rano looked up at Channo without answering. Channo continued: 'This old woman, Jindan—your mother-in-law—she will not let you live in peace; she will not let you be mistress of the house. There is only one way you can do it.'

'How?'

'You should marry Mangal; let him take you under his mantle.'

'Never!' exclaimed Rano as she stood up. 'You do not know what you are saying.'

'I am telling you the right thing to do. When the elder brother dies . . . .'

'Never, never never . . . ' repeated Rano. An angry shiver ran down her body. 'Mangal is a child. I brought him up as my own son. He is at least ten if not twelve years younger than I . . . I cannot think of it.' Rano ran back to her house.

When Rano came in, Mangal was bringing fodder for the horse. She glanced at the boy and screamed, 'Never, never, never!' and went indoors. She threw herself on her charpoy, covered her face and began to cry.

A little later Mangal came in with the harness. He wanted to get away earlier to earn more money. There was no rice in the house. He wanted to be able to buy flour, so that they could bake thick chapattis—the sort they used to bake in earlier days. Those chapattis were the only things that really filled a peasant's belly. Rice was like piddle; it went the way piddle did, leaving one as hungry as before. If he could find some vegetable to go with the chapattis, nothing could be better. The thought made Mangal drool at the mouth. If he could not get vegetables, an onion or some garlic would have to do. Vidya was sure to send some buttermilk. A little pepper and salt in the buttermilk to wash down the chapattis! Mangal smacked his lips in anticipation of the imaginary feast. He held the trappings in his hand and demanded: 'Rano, where is the horse's plume?'

Rano woke with a start. She stared at Mangal and then turned her face the other way. 'The children are at school.'

Mangal was nonplussed. 'That's the limit! I ask you for the feather plume which goes on the horse's head and you tell me about the children!' To make sure that his sister-in-law was well he came closer and touched her. Rano shrank back and screamed, 'Don't you dare touch me!'

Mangal withdrew his hand and examined his fingers. He found the plume he was looking for and fixed it on the harness. 'I am surprised that anyone as sensible as you should refuse to overlook what happened last night,' he said as he went out.

Rano went to the door and watched Mangal's retreating figure till it disappeared round the corner of the lane. She heard him sing a couplet from Warris Shah's *Heer-Ranjah*:

Said Heer to the wandering hermit: 'Your promises are a pack of lies.
'Is there anyone who can bring together lovers who have quarrelled?
Much have I sought and have tired of seeking
One who could bring back parted lovers to a lovers' meeting.'

Three

Channo spoke to Pooran Dei; Pooran Dei had a word with her husband, Gyan Chand, who was the sarpanch and at the time was engaged in settling some dispute regarding the village common, which he was also having levelled. 'I agree. That is as it ought to be,' he opined. 'Where else can poor Rano go to?' He paused for a while and asked, 'Isn't Mangal much younger than her?' 'What difference does that make?' replied his wife. 'As if there was a houri or a Heer waiting to marry him! They have hardly enough to eat; hardly any clothes to wear. It will solve two problems at a go. It will be the best thing for both of them.' To overawe her husband she came and stood beside him. 'Have you heard of the goings on between Mangal and that Salamat?' she demanded.

'No! What's going on between them?'

'If I had my way I would throw all the Muslim weavers out of the village. This Jhelum and her three daughters, they are a law unto themselves. The married one is no different from the unmarried. They behave like bitches on heat.'

'You go on muttering about other things. Will you tell me what has happened?' he demanded impatiently. 'Have they done anything wrong?'

'Not yet, but for sure they will by tomorrow or the day after.'

Gyan Chand had expected to hear something more exciting; he was visibly disappointed. Nevertheless he adopted a tone of warning: 'If they do anything wrong, they will meet the fate of Chaudhry Meharban Das and that "ascetic" with the steel loin-cloth, the so-called saint, Hari Das.'

Pooran Dei lowered her eyes. Gyan Chand's speech was pregnant with threats. 'If such things take place, women should know that it won't only be the men who have to pay the price. As long as women did not clamour for equality, they could be forgiven, but no longer.'

'I'd like to ask you one thing,' demanded Pooran Dei. 'Why did you send for Jhelum to the temple?' She was still churning up the Hari Das poison in her mind.

'We never asked her to come to the temple. It was to Mehr Karam Deen's garden,' replied Gyan Chand, a little out of breath. 'How could she as a Muslim come to the temple?'

'I see . . . instead of the temple, now it is Karmoo's garden,' commented Pooran Dei.

'Don't be crazy! She stole all the bananas in the garden.'

'What about the banana in your garden?'

'Mine was well fenced off,' smiled Gyan Chand, stroking his whiskers. 'Otherwise she would have had a good try.'

'Was it really well fenced? Or had straying cattle already had their fill?'

The blood drained from Gyan Chand's face. He tried to avoid Pooran's gaze and change the subject. 'Well, what about this business of Mangal's you wanted to discuss?'

'Not about Mangal, about Rano,' corrected Pooran Dei.

'All right, about Rano. I am of the opinion that he should take Rano under his mantle. Why should a woman brought to our village have to go to another? Why should we have to look around for other men? This sort of thing can bring a bad name to the village and its menfolk.'

He raised his head and shouted to the men at work, 'Hey, you young lads! Make sure the ground is level! See that you leave no holes!'

The workmen went on with their spades. Their well-oiled muscles glistened in the sunlight. It crossed Gyan Chand's mind that since the Punjab was short of women why should the men be denied access to the few who were available? Why should any woman be allowed to remain a shrivelled-up spinster? He went on his way to meet the villagers—first the elders and thereafter the Bhatias, the clan to which Mangal belonged.

While Mangal was away, some strangers came to see Waddi. Waddi did not know who they were and why they had come. But she obeyed her grandmother and went to Channo's for some fudge (more sugar than almonds!) to serve to the visitors. They were three men. One was middle-aged and the other two young, of whom one appeared to be the old man's son. Grandma Jindan nodded towards Waddi as she came out of the room. They looked her over as if she were a mare for sale. The young men were a little bashful, but the old man fastened his eyes on the girl like a leech. When Waddi sat down on her haunches to take water from the pitcher, the old man examined the ample spread of the girl's buttocks. 'Yes,' he drawled slowly, 'she'll do. She will do nicely.'

A sudden thought flashed across Waddi's mind and her forehead wrinkled. Before her grandmother could make any signs to her, the girl had run out of the house. She left behind a fragrance which only a young girl can exude.

Old Jindan started by demanding Rs. 1,000. The bargain was concluded for Rs. 550. The men were satisfied; they went away to give Jindan time to think it over. The hag had chosen a time when Rano was out picking cotton. Now she had to devise a means of getting the money from the men and handing over the girl to them. She knew that, despite her dismissal of Rano as a member of the household, she would have to get Rano's consent to the deal.

*

Jindan turned all her wiles on Rano when she came back. She put her withered arms about her waist and made her sit beside her. 'You were always destined to be my daughter-in-law,' she started. Rano saw through the game. Waddi emerged into the courtyard and gestured to her mother to come into the room. Old Grandma's eyes were too weak to catch the exchange of glances between the two women. Rano went to her daughter. Waddi told her what she had overheard, including the sum settled. (She had hidden herself behind the wall and overheard the deal.)

Rano flared up. She brushed aside her daughter and ran to face Jindan. She threw caution to the winds. She forgot her place and status. She was like an angry hen which, when its chicks are in danger, will fight a hawk to the death. 'Who were the men who came here today? Who had the audacity to enter my courtyard and bargain for the sale of my daughter?' she roared.

Jindan was beaten before the fray began. 'Daughter Rano, they were simply talking. One cannot stuff people's mouths, can one?'

'Of course you can! You can stuff their mouths and burn their tongues!' Rano was in no mood to listen to anything. 'You could have cut off the tongues of those bastards. You could have rammed a burning faggot in their mouths. My daughter—each one of her arms, every finger on her hand is worth a lakh of rupees!'

'Your daughter bears some relationship to me

as well,' protested Jindan. 'She is my granddaughter.'

'If you had a daughter-in-law you would have had a granddaughter. You have no daughter-in-law.' Rano began to scream. 'Don't you dare!' she went on screaming as she ran indoors. She flung herself on her charpoy. '*Hai*, am I fated to see my daughter sold? I brought nothing with me, so they treated me badly. And my child is to be sold for money.... They will break her bones, gnaw at her flesh. They'll taunt her: "We did not get you the way other people acquire wives; we had to pay money for you." '

When her husband, Tiloka, was alive, this used to be Rano's ultimate argument: 'If I did not bring anything with me, you did not have to pay anything to buy me! Remember! You married me, you did not purchase me .... ' 'And they'll sell my daughter. There's not enough to eat: how can we afford to have a wedding ceremony performed?' Then a sudden thought flashed across her mind. 'If Meharban Das Chaudhry was here, I would have provided for the dowry in one night. Then I could have afforded to entertain the bridegroom's party with the music of the shehnai, with dancing and singing. I could have entrusted my daughter to a proper bridegroom, with the *sehra* (veil) covering his handsome face. I could have put her in a palanquin and watched her depart through my tears. I could have cried, but I need not have admitted: "Daughter! For your future happiness your mother had to sell her honour for one night."

'And if the old hag got Rs. 500 (or was it Rs. 550?) she would hardly give me any part of it. If the girl has to be sold, why just Rs. 550 once for all? Why should I not take her to the bazaar and sell her piecemeal. There are hundreds of babu gentlemen loitering about the bazaars of Lahore who are willing to pay Rs. 15 or Rs. 20 for a moment's pleasure. We will get plenty to eat, and silks to wear . . . and brocades . . . and in a few days our trunks will be bursting with money and clothes.'

Rano woke from her reverie with a start. She heard the thwack of a slap. She had slapped her own face. And then, as often happened to her, she was gripped by an unknown fear and began to shiver.

*

Jindan was still considering the impact of Rano's remark, 'You can only have a granddaughter if you have a daughter-in-law,' when a party of villagers, including Gyan Chand, Kesar Singh, Jaggo, Dulla and Karam Deen, came in and sat around Hazoor Singh's charpoy. They beckoned to Jindan. They brought up the topic of Rano's being taken under Mangal's protection as casually as if they were the Panchayat dealing with the problem of filling up pits in the village common.

Hazoor Singh took offence. He felt that when he was nearing the end of his days, the Panchayat and his clansmen had come to insult him by giving him a parting kick. But with the nimble-minded

Jindan matters were quickly settled. Jindan only wondered (but for no more than a fleeting moment) why she had not herself thought of hitching Rano to Mangal. When poor Hazoor Singh blinked his bleary eyes at the village elders, Jindan ground her teeth and hissed, 'You keep out of this, old man! You can't get up from the charpoy; nor die on it. Do you know the evil that is going on in the world? You have been blind in this life; you'll remain blind in the life to come.'

After sounding out the old couple, the village elders took their leave. Jindan, in virtue of her age, gave them her blessing. The elders had barely turned their backs when Rano came out looking like a thundercloud. 'It was Waddi you were fixing up, you old busybody,' she snarled. 'Why are you now exhuming my corpse? If you have the least bit of shame left in you, take some poison and kill yourself! O Mother Goddess, drown this hag in the village cesspool! Let her bones be ground in the flour mill while the engine blasts *kooh kooh* . . . . Hag, why don't you lie with my little Chummoo? Why don't you become Banta's mistress? Do you think I will marry someone I gave my breast to . . . ?'

An unseen hand struck Rano on the head. She collapsed on the heap of garbage by the wall. When she came to she saw Channo standing above her. 'Slut! Husband-devouring witch! Kill yourself!' she hissed, grinding her teeth. Channo caught Rano by the hair and dragged her into the open lot at the back of the house which was used as a night rendezvous by the village lads and lasses. 'We try to do our best by you and, bitch that you are, you reward us by biting our hands.'

'No, no, Channo!' wailed Rano as she grabbed Channo by the feet. 'He is a child. I've never seen him with eyes of lust.'

Channo's tone became softer. 'Look, do you or don't you want to live in this village? Don't you have to pay the price for a full belly in this world? Don't you want to cover your shame? A great one you are to talk of eyes of lust! Bulhey Shah has said:

> *O Bulhey, the Almighty does not bother*
> *To uproot from one place and plant in another.*

That's all there is to it: take away from one and give to another. If you have not looked on him with eyes of lust, you can do so now, accursed one!'

Nothing was going to stop Channo: 'Just think how many women get two husbands in a lifetime! Once married and it's forever the same man. And if you have an affair or two and get into trouble, how will that be? Each time you do it you'll be terrified of the consequences. It's different for a man. It is a man's world. No one minds what they do. If an outsider can have Mangal, why not you? Have you heard of Salamat? Let's not talk about her. But surely you want your daughter to have henna on her palms and get married!'

Rano started up with a jerk. Was the woman talking of her marriage or her daughter's? Of course, it was hers! She became as stubborn as a child. 'No, no, no!' she repeated.

For the rest of the day Rano remained lost in her thoughts. A new conflagration had started in her body. This had nothing to do with Waddi, nor with the twins, nor even with the baby. It was like the quickening of a new child in her womb.

When Pooran Dei came to see her in the evening, Rano had fever. She had tied a rag round her head. Channo applied a poultice made in the form of birds to her forehead. The 'birds' were pecking at Rano's troubles. Pooran Dei first enquired about her health. Then she asked again with a meaningful smile, 'What kind of fever is this?' Rano smiled and turned her back on Pooran Dei.

Thus was desire rekindled in Rano's body. Pooran Dei laughed. Waddi could not comprehend what was going on; nevertheless she felt it was too good an occasion to miss and readily joined the other two women in the banter and jesting. Her shrill laughter scattered the parakeets on the neem tree. The sun scattered its last drops of vermilion over the spire of the temple. And the bells began to chime for the evening worship.

Mangal suddenly came in and planted himself on the threshold. He looked pleased with himself and with life. He had earned seven rupees. And as usual the first thing he did was to place the money in Rano's hands. Pooran Dei blurted out: 'Well, here it is! His first earnings. May he ever earn for you to spend!'

Rano let the money slip out of her palms. The notes scattered in the breeze; the coins rolled on to the plastered floor. Mangal asked in a tone of surprise, 'What is the joke, Aunty?'

'Ask this woman of yours,' replied Pooran Dei. She dragged Waddi away with her, leaving poor Rano with Mangal.

Mangal broke into an asinine laugh: 'All the women of Kotla need is....'

'Are the men any different?' interrupted Rano.

Mangal was puzzled. He went inside and got out a nice new shirt from his trunk; the shirt had been brought by him from Peshawar. It was embroidered round the collar with apricot flowers. As he aired the shirt he remarked, 'One can at least make some sense of what men say or do.'

'Men understand other men; women understand women,' replied Rano, with a mischievous twinkle in her eyes—a twinkle which women have known how to produce since the days of Adam. Mangal pondered over her words and felt that there was truth in what she said. Perhaps Rano knew instinctively that under the cover of the dark night and in the seclusion of the vacant lot where the Chaudhry stored building material he and Salamat would soon be sowing the seed of a new life. He turned round at the door and asked, 'Why have you picked up this man-*versus*-woman argument?'

'That is the crux of the whole problem.'

'Sounds as if it was a historic battle!'

'Older than history,' replied Rano, coming close to him. 'It's a battle in which the victor is vanquished and yet the loser remains the loser.'

Mangal paused in his footsteps and tried to

figure out the deep meaning behind Rano's words. Neither knew very much about the other; but it was one of those moments in life when the most meaningless of sentences becomes pregnant with meaning. And, of course, the most sensible remark can also sound as if it were absolute nonsense.

Whether or not their dialogue had any import, neither of them had the ability or the time to make sense of it. Rano was in her early thirties. She was a big-boned woman, in whose ample frame had been relit the flame of desire. Although she did not have the bashfulness of a virgin, she did have the pride of her sex and the longing to be desired. The desire had lain dormant for a long time; it had been submerged under the humdrum of life. Now it was bubbling over, bursting the bounds of discretion.... And on the other side was a strapping lad of twenty-four—a lusty youth with the world at his feet.

Rano came out into the courtyard and began to tinker with the kitchen utensils. The trick worked. Mangal did not go to his tryst with Salamat. Ma Jindan called to her son. Mangal went to her. She sent Waddi and the boys out of the house to play. She got Mangal to sit beside her and began to explain the situation. Rano slipped away and hid behind the door.

*

Jindan had barely broached the subject when Mangal realized what would follow. His hair seemed to pour out of his turban. He raised his turban with one hand, and with the index finger of the other began to push back his locks. In the light of the setting sun his face glowed a fiery red.

Rano leant against the wall and put her hand on her heart; she could hear it throb. It sounded like the thumping of the footsteps of a murderer running down the stairs after committing his foul deed. If anyone had seen her, he would have been reminded of a marrow come unseasonably into flower and, like the marrow flower, become sallow and withered. Her lips turned as dark as dried raisins. Her knees knocked. She was overcome by fear and by love.

Mangal rose and glanced in the direction where he believed Rano had gone. 'No, never! This can never take place.' He sawed the air with an air of finality, as though bringing down a whip on the horse's flanks to get it to break into a gallop. 'I am not going to be called a mother-seducer . . . . I will rape the mothers of those elders of the village! What the hell do I care for what they say? Even if Lord Irwin or George V came to ask me, I would say "No". She's old enough to be my mother. I can place my head at her feet, but not bed her.'

He raved and ranted; he cursed the air as he ran out. A shadow moved across the wall. 'Dear me!' screamed Jindan, 'Rano, you hot one—I hope he does not do something foolish. He went out swearing that the corpse of another Tiloka would be carried into the house.'

Rano leapt towards the front door. She stumbled, rose and staggered forward. Channo,

Pooran Dei, Vidya and the other women held her back. Rano tried to free herself. '*Hai*!' she groaned pointing into black space.

'He won't do anything,' said Channo firmly.

'*Hai*, if he comes to any harm, I'll kill myself. We'll all be dead—and all the blame will come on me,' wailed Rano.

'To hell with you!' snapped Vidya stepping to the fore. 'Who is there to blame except us?'

Rano put her hands to her bosom and leaned against Pooran Dei. 'Mother Goddess! I have turned as cold as death.'

Channo rubbed Rano's hands. 'We've created all this fuss to hot you up . . . and you reward us by turning into ice.'

'Aunty, save me!' cried Rano, grabbing Channo's feet.

Pooran Dei shook the girl away. 'Why are you killing yourself? Nothing will happen to you. Men are like horses. When you saddle them they kick their hind legs. If we women did not act as we do, we'd still be virgins. Surely you know that . . . .'

Rano picked up a little courage. She covered her face with the palms of her hands. She trembled as she spoke to Channo, 'What will he do?'

'He will come round to the idea—as you have.'

'What will he think?'

'The same as you; and then change his views.'

Waddi stood near by, listening to the conversation. She had some inkling of the affair. She spoke up, 'If Mother does anything of the kind, I'll take poison and kill myself.'

The women slapped their foreheads with their hands and cried, '*Hai*!' Channo caught Waddi by her pigtail and pushed her indoors. Waddi's face reflected hatred, shame and humiliation.

*

Salamat passed by Mangal's house and heard the squabbling, without getting any idea of what it was about. She came to her tryst. She had it in mind to recite the following couplet to Mangal when he came:

> *The happy sweetheart pined for the moon,*
> *But even her lover ceased to pass her way.*

She caught sight of Mangal; he seemed upset and angry. He came close to Salamat, then suddenly withdrew. Salamat went up to him and tried to make out the reason for his sullenness. She had worn all her finery: she had draped herself in her elder sister's wedding dupatta; its mica sparkled like silver. The soft evening breeze made the dupatta flutter in the breeze like the silver paper on a stick of candy.

Even in the dark Mangal's eyes glowed like torches. He planted one foot on a wooden beam, most of which had been hacked away for use as fuel. Mangal spoke with a heavy voice: 'Salamtey!'

'*Hoon*.'

'Come here.'

Salamat rose from her seat and came close to him.

'Take off that dupatta,' he ordered.

Salamat took off the dupatta and put it aside.

'Take off your shirt.'

Salamat took off her shirt—it is the hardest thing for a girl to do, but Salamat obeyed. She had lost her will power. She crossed her arms in front of her to hide her bosom and coyly lowered her head. Mangal saw what he had wanted to see in the dim light of a distant oil lamp. Before Salamat could say anything, he spoke in the same heavy voice: 'You've had your outing; now you can go home.'

The petrified Salamat hurriedly put her neck through her shirt, picked up her dupatta and, with many a frightened glance over her shoulder, ran back to her home.

Someone passed by and having nothing better to say to break the silence demanded, 'Who is there?'

Mangal lost his temper and swore: 'Son of a bitch! Get the hell out of here!' The man sensed danger and fled towards the village.

Mangal tarried for a while. He was lost in his thoughts. He then jerked his left arm as if lashing his whip and then started towards Salamat's house which was on the outskirts of the village. Here lived cobblers, washermen and other menials amid the stench of dung heaps and stagnant sewers.

Four

So arrived the day fixed by the elders of the village. Pooran, Channo and Vidya got together and daubed Rano's palms with henna. They combed and plaited her hair and rolled it into a bun. Despite the assurances and cajolery, Rano was scared and wept incessantly.

The twins did not comprehend what was going on and wondered what their mother was being put through. Waddi put her arm round her little brothers, but in trying to comfort them she upset them all the more. And later, as prearranged, all the children were sent away to the house of Aunty Channo.

In the courtyard they placed some pitchers. Above the pitchers they spread a somewhat soiled sheet of cambric and tied its ends between the neem tree and the steel bars of the fanlight. Beside the pitchers was an old, chipped, earthenware cup full of vermilion powder. They made Rano sit under the soiled sheet. As she took her seat, she whined: 'O thou who art dead and gone, see what they are doing to thy Rano!'

The priest demanded: 'Where is the groom?'

Pandit Gyan Chand, Kesar Singh and the other men present looked around. They had dragged Mangal to the house and tied his hands to the legs of a charpoy. Mehr Karam Deen, who had kept away, came in and announced, 'Mangloo is not here.'

A northern gale blew into the sheet; it fluttered wildly and beat a loud tattoo. The wooden birds tied to the sheet rattled. Dabboo who lay curled up on the heap of ashes by the oven got up and cocked his head to one side, then to the other. He was old and feeble and could not stand too much noise or glare. He looked at the comings and goings of the men and women and then decided to make a mild protest: 'Bow-wow!'

'I know the lad; he is bad seed,' exclaimed old Hazoor Singh.

'O fie!' hissed Jindan. 'The old fogey has nothing to do but stick his nose into other people's business.' She turned her bleary old eyes to the throng in her courtyard. She had no premonition of the calamity that was to befall them. Through the mist of her failing eyesight she saw the figure of her murdered son.

'Wait a moment, Brahmin,' commanded the

village headman. 'I'll fetch that lover-of-his-mother.'

'I'll come with you,' volunteered Kesar Singh.
'Let's all go to get him,' suggested Jaggo.
'What a fellow! After all the thrashing we gave him, he's still dared to run away!' said Diwana.

The villagers had already done their best to brainwash Mangal and put him on the right track. They were even willing to break Mangal's bones, so that he would not be able to move from under the sheet. Half a dozen men armed with staves and choppers went out to look for him. In deference to the law, Gyan Chand feigned to stop them by asking them to desist and then staying in the rear. Only the women remained in the courtyard. Amongst them was the midwife, Surma *dai*, who had helped at Mangal's birth.

When she saw the men go out armed, Rano began to beat her breast. 'Let me go! For God's sake set me free! This will kill me....' She fell in a faint. The women took water in palmfuls from the pitchers assembled for the wedding, poured it on Rano's mouth and splashed it on her face. They were determined to make her come round, so that she could witness her own wedding—just as she had, not very long ago, witnessed her widowing.

They found Mangal hiding in the seventh cotton field of the experimental farm. The earlier beating had dispirited him. The prospect of a second thrashing made him turn deathly pale. (If he had really wanted to get away he could have taken out his ekka on the road to Satraha or Sattoki. Was it fate that had destined he should be near his village and in a place where he could be found?)

Mangal hoped that his friends Gurdas, Nawab, Ismail and others would come to his rescue; he did not expect them to join the rest of the heartless crowd of Kotla. They kept assuring him, 'All said and done, it is not a matter of life-and-death for you; it's only a woman you have to face!'

A few yards from Mangal's hiding-place was the well near which Tiloka had been murdered. The evening had become dark before its time; the sun had sprinkled the leaves of the neem with blood. The earth still smelt of blood.

Mangal had chosen the darkest corner of the cotton field. When the villagers came he peered out of the dark with fear writ all over his face. During the winter months, hyenas and wild pigs were often found in the fields about Kotla. Villagers were known to surround the beasts and beat them to pulp with their staves and choppers.

The villagers came and formed a line in front of Mangal. Mangal sat huddled with his two hands resting on the ground; he fixed his pursuers with his haunted eyes. He was like a wild boar at bay. He was unarmed. They had bamboo poles in their hands. In the first encounter they had created a shindy that could be heard in the next village; and now they were taking up their positions in absolute silence. They looked into each other's eyes for a signal; they glowered at him; they waited for someone to make the first move and see in which direction their quarry would try to make a breakthrough.

Mangal's pulse beat violently. The men's hearts also beat violently. Mangal had cramp in his thigh and tried to change his stance. This was a signal for the men to go into action. Without a thought, they began to beat on the ground about them, raising clouds of dust. They stopped as suddenly as they had begun. The hunters and the hunted eyed each other in silence. Then Gurdas, the ekka-driving friend of Mangal, stepped in front and said, 'Let me see how tough this man is.'

Kesar Singh, Jaggo, Nawab and Ismail leapt behind Gurdas. Mangal got up and tried to break through the cordon. They fell on him from left, right and centre. Those who had staves used their staves; those who did not used their slippers. He knew that if he fought back too hard there were people armed with choppers.

They caught Mangal by his long hair, dragged, kicked and pushed him across the fields and footpaths. Being Sikhs themselves it was up to headman Tara Singh and Kesar Singh to prevent dishonour to Mangal's unshorn locks. But today these two men were the leaders of the gang and were both settling old scores as well as enjoying themselves. To save his being dragged by the hair, Mangal agreed to go along of his own accord. Then, like a mule reluctant to approach his trough of water, he dug in his heels—and the beating, pushing and kicking were resumed. His clothes were torn, his long hair and beard were covered with the fluff of cotton, thistledown and green burrs.

By the time they came to the pond by the

temple, it had become a sizeable procession. People collected by the roadside to witness the development. A woman passer-by raised the fence of thorns and enquired of a village maiden: '*Hai* Sukho, what on earth is going on here?'

Sukho looked at the woman and answered laconically, 'A wedding,' and turned away as if it was the most natural occurrence.

The top of Naina Devi was still visible in the gloom of the twilight. It was a full-moon night dedicated to Naina Devi; pilgrims circumambulating the peak were singing hymns to the accompaniment of drums and cymbals:

Save us sinners, Holy Mother Amba!
The time for Salvation is nigh.

The hymn-singers must surely have turned their faces towards the spiral of dust rising from Kotla and then looked away!

The village common had been levelled, save for one remaining pit. It was into this pit that Mangal stumbled and fell, to become unconscious. The pit had been dug by Jhelum's family to store water for their vegetable beds. (That was why Jhelum's beds were ever green and her vegetables always in season). There was also the gentle shade of the juniper which had comforted many a traveller; the cool breeze whistling through its leaves had lulled many a weary man to sleep. The Arains had dammed the overflow of water. Mangal's fall loosened the dam; the water began to flow out of the pond. Before they could pick him up, his clothes were drenched and caked with mud and filth. Mangal made many attempts to free himself, but he was one against ten of Kotla's toughest lads who held him as if in a vice. Mangal gave up the struggle and went along like a noisy drunkard.

It was an odd kind of bridegroom! No turban on his head and his hair scattered all over his face. Into his grip they forced a blunted kirpan. And instead of the *sehra* — veil of flowers — there were thorns and thistles; instead of saffron he was daubed with mud; in his eyes instead of love were hate, frustration and defeat. And what an odd assortment of rustics to make up the bridegroom's party—almost like Shiva come to wed his Parvati! Twined about his neck with the serpent was the *rudrakshamala*; a cup of hashish was at his lips, a tight loin-cloth over his sex, a deer-skin was his floor-mat and a trident was in his hand. And monkeys, langurs, tigers, leopards and elephants formed his wedding party. To cap it all there was the 'music'—not the shehnai, as at other weddings, but the buzz of a myriad flies and the piercing *kooh, kooh* of the flourmill.

When Mangal took his seat on the wedding stool he was covered with blood. Rano was unconscious. But the women of the village knew that it would all end well. Although the ceremony of the sheet is neither very long nor very involved, Channo, Pooran Dei, Vidya and Kooki had got together the paraphernalia for a regular wedding and were reluctant to let it go waste. Usually, it is the bridegroom who goes to the home of the bride to marry her, but since the bride's parental home and the husband's were the same, the women decided to divide themselves into two parties. Pooran Dei, Vidya and a few others pretended to belong to Rano's parental home. Jindan, Channo, Sarupo, Chandi and Surma represented the bridegroom. The groups sat in two rows facing each other. As the mother of the bridegroom, Jindan took the lead in singing the *ghori*:

> *Tiny little droplets*
> *A gentle shower of rain:*
> *Blessed be the mother*
> *Who sees her son married!*

Jindan gestured to Channo, Sarupo and Surma. They sung the following lines in chorus:

> *Blessed the sister*
> *Who leads thy horse to the bride's home.*
> *Blessed the brother's wife*
> *Who puts antimony in thine eyes.*
> *May thy father carry a sackful of gold.*

Waddi came up on to the roof-top to see the goings-on; she had her little brothers with her. When little Chummoo had wanted to see the fun, Waddi had slapped him. But now Waddi herself could not resist the temptation. As soon as she came out onto Aunty Channo's roof-top, her brothers followed her. The children witnessed the marriage of their own mother. At first Waddi shed bitter tears; then the child in her won the day. She forgot her sorrow and came down to join the crowd.

Vidya shouted at the others: 'Girls, why don't you sing?' The women extended their necks and began to sing for all they were worth. Headman Tara Singh, Gyan Chand, Diwana, Kesar Singh, Jaggo, Ruldu, Dulla, Jamala, and the menials who watched from a respectable distance shouted: 'Go on ladies, sing!'

Meanwhile Rano came to and began to stare with uncomprehending eyes at the men and women surrounding her. Vidya took a couplet from an old song and improvised lines to suit the occasion:

May your horse have lentils yellow and gold!
Little boy, may your father carry sacks of gold!
Little boy, may your sister lead your horse on your wedding day!

It was now for the bride's party to reply. Pooran Dei intoned a song of marital bliss referring to her days with her 'princely' father:

Father dear, you love to sleep.
You have to find a husband for your unmarried daughter.
She asks for a handsome bridegroom.
She asks for a comfortable home.

Someone put his hand against his mouth and produced the sound of a trumpet. It indicated that the bridegroom's party had arrived. Then came the high moment of the ceremony and everyone was transfixed wherever he or she, old or young, happened to be—whether in the open, on the parapet of the well, on the roof-top, or in the branch of a tree. Pooran Dei and her sharp-tongued friend, Vidya faced the bridegroom's party and let fly a shower of abuse: 'Monkeys . . . pigs . . . bastards!' and much else. As the women uttered these imprecations they occasionally pointed to their husbands. Everyone was roaring with laughter. The women began to dance. Pooran Dei raised her arm. (The men of Kotla have never forgotten the English bra over her full bosom!) She exchanged a bawdy verse with Vidya. Then Nawab's wife Ayesha, and Jhelum Arain with her three daughters, Ayesha, Inayat and Salamat, joined the others in dancing and singing.

The men joined in the laughter and games—everyone joined, old as well as young. Men pulled the girls' plaits, put their arms round the waists of strangers. No one cared. The Brahmin Pooran Dei fell into the arms of the Muslim, Jamal, and pretended to pass out in a swoon. Vidya and Sarupo were intertwined. Somebody gave Waddi such a violent push that she found herself in the lap of Gyan Chand—who promptly took her in his loving embrace.

The sheet was pulled away; the nuptials were over. Everyone stood up in silence. It was time for the bride to sit in her palanquin and leave her 'parental' home. The bride's relatives began a song of farewell:

Father, you have no claim; the groom's father has his hand on the palanquin: she has become his daughter.
Brother, you have no claim; the groom's brother has his hand on the palanquin: she has become his sister-in-law.
I, the bride, leave my dolls in the niche; I do not want to play with them any more.
My friends have come to see me off; I have no wish to see them.
Hai my mother's tears have drenched her shirt; my father is in a flood of tears.

Then there was the ceremony of the bride showing her face.

They pushed Rano and Mangal into a room and locked it from the outside.

*

Rano spent her wedding night treating Mangal's bruises; she treated him as if she were his sister, wife and mother in one. Since she could not go out of the room to the kitchen, she warmed her dupatta with her breath and pressed it on Mangal's contusions. Mangal continued to groan. Sometimes, when the pain receded, he thought of the gentle hands that were caressing him. The red of the henna on Rano's palms glowed in the dark; a strange fragrance like that of lemon blossoms when winter turns to spring came to his nostrils.

Had Rano completely forgotten the existence of

her children? Who had put them to bed? Had someone given them something to eat before they fell asleep? Little Chummoo's face flashed before her mental vision—and as suddenly disappeared. In any case what had happened that day was beyond the child's comprehension, so why bother!

Mangal turned on his side; Rano shifted to make place for him. Suddenly she felt very thirsty. She could not bring herself to open the window and ask for water. Mangal also got up and began groping in the dark. In a fit of frenzy, he tore up the remaining shreds of his tattered shirt.

'I wish I were dead!' exclaimed Rano as she came and sat beside him.

'Begone . . . . Drop dead!' swore Mangal as he pushed her away violently.

Only a quarter of the night remained.

Rano put her head between Mangal's feet and began to cry. 'You know I had nothing to do with this.'

'I know,' Mangal replied. His eyes had become accustomed to the dark and he could see her. Rano did not withdraw the hand that he took in his. Would this man whose fate had joined him to her jerk away his calloused hands in the same way that he jerked them when he used his whip? With baited breath she awaited his next move. Mangal's grip loosened; their hands fell apart. And then they both fell asleep on their respective charpoys.

People believed that marriage was one long wedding night. Most of them did not have a clue;

many had forgotten their own experience. The warmth of the nuptial bed is tepid in comparison to the warmth and excitement and fulfilment true marriage engenders in the hearts of a couple. Copulation is counterfeit; it is the let down a needy man feels when he abandons his self-respect and stretches his hand to beg from someone he believes to be a generous millionaire—and that man awards him with a measly copper.

When they awoke in the morning they found their door unlocked. Mangal stood up and tried to take a step. His legs were stiff and a sharp pain racked his body. He fell back on his charpoy. Rano went out into the courtyard where Jindan was sitting.

'Daughter, what do you want?' asked Jindan.

'Give me the key to the store, Mother.'

'What for?'

'I want to get some turmeric; he is badly hurt.'

Jindan fished out the bunch of keys from her dupatta and gave it to Rano. Instead of going to the store, Rano first went to see her children sleeping on the veranda. It was cold and they lay half-naked and huddled together to keep warm. Rano kissed them in turn, took the tangled sheets from their legs and covered them properly. The children stretched their limbs and continued to slumber. Only Waddi did not go back to sleep. When Rano bent down to kiss her, the girl clawed at her mother's face with nails which she grew like a modern city girl's. 'Go away!' she spat angrily. 'Go and blacken your face with that fellow!'

Rano had suffered enough; her daughter's behaviour was the unkindest cut of all, particularly as it was for her children's sake that she had agreed to marry Mangal. But Rano swallowed her pride and her shame and without a word went into the larder. She made a poultice on the heating iron and took it in to Mangal. Mangal was gone. Rano came out. He was not in the courtyard. Dabboo came up to her whining and wagging his tail. He put his forelegs on her as if he wanted to comfort her: 'I know what you have suffered; but it will pass and all will be well again.'

*

Channo went to the temple every morning. In winter her tremulous voice chanting prayers could be heard from a great distance. That morning, instead of going to the temple, Channo came to see Rano. Rano was standing at her door.

'Rano, I hope all is well with you.'

Rano did not answer.

'I am your friend. Why don't you tell me?'

Rano remained silent.

'For God's sake, say something!' exploded Channo. 'Did anything happen last night? *Hai* . . . how you have sealed your lips!'

Rano looked down at the ground. Her lips quivered. 'No . . . nothing.'

Channo scanned Rano's face. 'You are lying! How did you come by those nail-marks on your face?'

Large tears rolled down Rano's cheeks. Shame and sorrow pressed heavy on her. Suddenly she flared up and exploded, 'This thing you talk about, I don't want it .... Sister, all I ask is a rag to cover my nakedness and a couple of chapattis to appease my hunger. But who knows the will of God, or the wish of the Mother Goddess, Vaishno Devi? He has wandered off again.'

'*Hai* Ram!' exclaimed Channo, as she peered into the grey light of the dawn. 'Where on earth can the wretch have gone?' Channo suddenly realized she should not use such language. 'May my mouth be burnt! I should not be speaking like this in front of you.'

Rano smiled.

'Don't worry about him, Rano,' said Channo, trying to reassure her friend. 'Your good man will come back the same way he went.'

And so it was; by noon Mangal was back. He had borrowed a shirt from Nawab, a turban from Gurdas and a fancy pair of upturned slippers from Ismail. His injuries had been properly bandaged. He had not much faith in home remedies and had taken a lift in Ismail's tonga and had himself attended to at the General Hospital at Daska. God alone knew whether he had had anything to eat that morning. And all he had had the day earlier had been a sound thrashing.

Mangal spent the whole day on his charpoy snapping twigs between his fingers. At times he felt himself as light as a feather; and immediately afterwards he felt the weight of the whole world on his shoulders. Then he would start doodling on the ground. Suddenly he would stand up and irritably rub out the doodles with the palms of his hands. Then he would pass the same hands unwittingly over his face and cover it with dust. He raised his hand to shoo away a raven which was hoarsely cawing in the neem tree; then made a menacing gesture towards a mangy pye-dog. Half a dozen dogs came round the corner snarling and snapping at each other. Mangal tried to drive them away. 'I would not be a bit surprised to know that the people of Kotla when they died turned into dogs!' he said bitterly.

Far away from the house shone the glittering ranges of the Dhauladhar and Himalayas. They met at points, merged into each other, and then parted in different directions. On the other side of the hills was the land known since time immemorial as the 'land of despair': the land where lovers were destined never to meet, but faced each other, on opposite hills, separated by a river. So it was sung:

> *The mountain-dwellers are sinners.*
> *Their hearts are made of stone.*
> *Their eyes meet daily —*
> *But their bodies, never.*

Mangal reminisced over past happenings. He sighed, then began to hum the complaint of Mirza to his beloved, Sahiban:

O Sahiban, you did me a grievous wrong.
You tied my hands,
Hid my bow and quiver.
Had I been free
With one arrow would I have pierced
your brother's bodies
And with another
Pierced the breast of your loved one.

The song did not soothe his feelings. So he sang another one more mournful:

(A peasant woman pleads with Faqir Chhuttan Shah:)
O Shah, I'll sacrifice a goat at thy tomb
If you take away my husband;
Destroy some of my neighbours' wives,
And smite with sickness those that remain.
Let the village headman, who reports to the police, have a fit;
Let the bania's shop, where a lamp is always alight, be burnt to ashes;
Let the faqir's bitch, who barks day and night to keep a vigil, perish,
And let all the lanes leading to my house be empty.
So may my beloved Mirza come to me—
(without fear of husbands, wives, headmen, tradesmen and barking dogs).

Mangal felt better. He went in and lay down on his charpoy. The ill-temper had drained out of his system and he was at peace with himself.

Rano quickly cooked a meal. She took ghee from Channo and, like a dutiful wife, smothered the chapattis for her husband with the clarified butter. She fetched a clove of garlic and was about to rub it on the chapattis when a thought crossed her mind. She blushed—and put away the garlic.

She arranged the chapattis and vegetables in a brass plate and ordered Waddi: 'Go and serve him.'

Waddi's nostrils widened. She shrugged her shoulders and replied: 'I'll serve him with a pair of slippers.'

Rano held back the tears that welled up in her eyes. Fortunately Chummoo intervened: 'Give me the salver; I'll take it to him.'

Rano looked up at her son. Did the child understand her predicament? Or was his innocence beyond passing judgement on the conduct of other people? Rano had a strong urge to take her child in her embrace and crush him to her bosom till he became part of her and would never again have to suffer the slights of the world. She pushed the brass plate in front of Chummoo, and when he was gone, she took a piece of her veil between her teeth and began to cry.

*

So passed many days and many months. Mangal became aware of his family responsibilities. Very seldom did he return home with less than five rupees. Although he did not consummate his marriage with Rano, he gave his earnings to her and not to his mother. This made Rano both happy and depressed. The nagging of the village women had aroused physical desire in her. Channo, Pooran Dei, Vidya, Sarupo—just about everyone—asked her, 'Has he done anything to you yet?'

Rano was fed up of hearing the question. All she could do was to swear and reply, 'Sluts! Can't you see I am grateful for having a roof over my head? No one can now turn me out of my house. No one can sell my daughter. Isn't that enough?'

The women were like wasps on a bag of sugar. They buzzed about her; they dug their hands into her waist and said, 'Don't tell us that he lies beside you all night without doing anything!'

'Yes.'

'You on one charpoy, he on another?'

'That's right.'

'And you haven't the courage to say or do anything?'

'No.'

'Why not? He is your man; he has taken you under his mantle.'

Rano was often on the verge of tears. 'What if he has spread his sheet over me? To me he is no different from what he used to be.'

The women were astounded. 'Fie! Shame on you! Have your face blackened! How can you get sleep without . . . ?'

'Just as I used to before I married him.'

'And he? Does he doze off without doing anything?'

'Yes.'

'Doesn't he get up during the night? Doesn't he stretch his limbs or yawn or . . . ?' The women would burst out laughing and dig each other in the ribs. Then they would add words of caution. 'You must do something about it or you'll lose your man.'

'If you like, I can get her a charm or an amulet,' suggested Pooran Dei.

'Why not!' agreed Vidya.

'No, never!' exclaimed Rano. 'I will not have anything to do with love potions and the like.'

'If you are not willing to wear a charm, you will have to spend the rest of your days in tears,' warned Pooran Dei.

Vidya turned to Pooran Dei and said in meaningful tones, 'I take it you don't have to shed any tears.'

Pooran Dei flared up. She pointed to her slippers and rasped, 'My slippers do the crying! If I hadn't got that charm, I wouldn't have had my Shambhu. And my husband would have thrown me out of the house.'

The women shrieked with laughter; their teeth looked like a field of cotton in flower. Channo winked at her companions and asked Pooran Dei, 'How long did you have to spend with Baba Hari Das?'

Pooran Dei caught Channo by her pigtail and screamed: 'This will be the death of me!' They began to quarrel, and then the gathering broke up.

Meanwhile, at the Naseebanwala tonga-stand Gurdas, Nawab and Ismail pestered Mangal. 'Well, how did you find her?' Mangal's face turned scarlet—as if someone had insinuated that he was having an incestuous affair with his mother or sister. He said nothing but busied himself tightening the belt round his horse and then patting it. Gurdas took the matter a step further: 'If you ask my opinion, an experienced woman is great fun.'

'What kind of fun?' enquired Nawab or Ismail, to keep the topic alive.

'She's been broken in; she knows all the tricks.'

They laughed. Mangal's angry voice interrupted their laughter: 'You bastards! I'll break in your mothers!'

They eyed Mangal with silent hostility. Only Gurdas dared to say anything more—he was stronger than any of the others; one had to think twice before picking a quarrel with Gurdas: '*Oi* Mangla, did you marry Rano to adopt her as your Mama?'

Mangal returned Gurdas's hostile look but considered discretion the better part of valour. When the unpleasantness was dissipated, Ismail changed the subject: 'A Sikh sardar lost an anna coin in his hearth.'

'What did he do about it?' asked Nawab, eyeing Mangal. Then a woman passed by and Nawab asked her, '*Mai*, do you want to go to Kotla?''

'No, brother,' she replied and went on her way. Nawab turned to Ismail and repeated, 'And what did the Sikh sardar do about the anna he lost in the hearth?'

'Oh yes,' replied Ismail. 'Without taking off his *kuccha* the Sikh leapt into the hearth to look for his coin. He raised his hands to the heavens and began to cry, 'Allah, help me find my coin!' A Muslim happened to pass by. He was surprised to hear a Sikh pray to Allah. '*Oi* Sikha, why do you invoke the help of our Allah and not of your own Guru?' asked the Muslim. The Sikh peered over the rim of the oven and replied, 'You think I would be so foolish as to have my Guru inside a hot oven to find one miserable anna?'

The tongawallahs went into fits of laughter and slapped each other's hands. Even Mangal began to smile. Ismail treated Mangal's smile as a permit for further licence. 'Mangla, is it true that at twelve o'clock the Sikhs lose their senses?'

'Yes, it is true.'

'Really! Do you lose your wits at twelve?'

'*Aho* — I too.'

Ismail placed his hand on Mangal's top-knot and asked, 'Do you feel something here?'

'Yes, I do,' replied Mangal.

That was not enough for Ismail. He persisted, 'Is it only twelve o'clock in the afternoon or also twelve midnight which affects you people in that way?'

'Afternoon . . . . A proper Sikh only feels it at noon. It's the intense heat . . . the long hair . . . the turban.'

'And what happens to that Basakha Singh, the carpenter of our village?' demanded Ismail. 'He gets very rowdy at midnight.'

'That bastard must be a Muslim convert to Sikhism.'

Five

The ekka-drivers were roaring with laughter. Mangal's laughter was the loudest. The laughter died down as a couple came their way. The drivers pounced on them. Soon the woman's bundle was in Nawab's ekka, her slippers in Mangal's, and she herself in Gurdas' arms. The poor husband was hustled into another ekka. The ekka-drivers swore at each other. Then they put the man and wife in one ekka and sent them off.

Mangal's only interest in women now was as passengers. If his eyes fell on a pretty wench, he would casually glance at her as much as to say, 'I suppose this kind also exists.' Salamat was the only exception. From the women's gossip Salamat had got to know that nothing had happened between Mangal and his wife. So she became even more provocative in her dress and walk when she passed by Mangal. Although she threw many an inviting glance at Mangal, inside her she was really full of anger and hate. She had sworn to inveigle Mangal to the same vacant lot where he had insulted her, make him take off his clothes and, when he made a move towards her, start screaming. She would humiliate him in public and in a manner that no one would ever forget. And now that he had a wife, it would give her something to taunt him with for the rest of his days.

One day at the ekka-stand Mangal met Nawab and the two took some liquor. He did not enjoy it, for he drank with some trepidation in his heart. When his brother was alive he could empty a bottle by himself. Now fear gnawed inside him. He wanted to drink and at the same time he was afraid of the consequences.

Rano was one of those intuitive types who watch every expression on the faces of their men and read their moods from the lines on their foreheads. If their men have been unfaithful, their instinct tells them. They can tell from the tone of voice; even the walk is enough. They can read their menfolk like an open book. Mangal was in the habit of taking an occasional drink. Rano knew that. Mangal knew that Rano knew. On the subject of drink, however, the veil of silence was never lifted and life was peaceful.

As the days went by, the women became more aggressive towards Rano. Rano began to feel that there might be some truth in what they said. She became anxious about her future and the future of her children. Mangal often became irritable and burst out: 'What's all this caboodle? I don't want to have anything to do with it.' It terrified Rano. She could say nothing to him. What right had she to say anything—or did she have a right? . . . After all, the ceremony had taken place in the presence of the elders, her kinsmen and the women of the village. Perhaps she had some right over him—even if not a very strong one. What after all is a sheet? A rag three yards long, no more! But then what more is there to circumambulating round the Granth?

There was this difference, that although she had been scared of Tiloka, she had never hesitated to say what came to her mind and to raise Cain—even if he thrashed her for her pains. Why couldn't she say anything to Mangal? He did not raise his little finger to her. Except at night, when he was forced to share a room with her, he did not even come near her.

One day Mangal came home while it was still daylight. The light in the sky made the moon appear like a pale kite caught in the branches of the keekar tree. The moon raced along the sky keeping pace with Mangal's ekka and then came to a halt above the spot where Mangal drew up. Mangal unharnessed the horse and gave it its feed before going home. He came back and gave the horse a brushing.

Mangal stabled the horse and put away the ekka before he went in. Not far from where he left his ekka was the experimental farm with its sugar-cane standing high, as solid as a wall; only the spiders wove their gossamer between the stalks. Beyond the field was the village school and next to it the home of the Arain woman, Jhelum. Beyond Jhelum's home was the moon.

A strange odour pervaded the atmosphere. Mangal's nostrils were familiar with the smell. It was the time of year when the peasants crushed cane. And after they had drunk the juice and stacked the cakes of gur, they filled earthen pots with jaggery, added the green bark of the keekar to it and buried the pots in dung-heaps. Within a few days the stuff would begin to ferment; a pleasant gurgle would rise from the bottom and bubbles burst on its surface. It was drained into other earthenware pots, or bottled. The air caught the odour of fermenting cane and wafted it across the village.

Summer was turning to autumn. People accustomed to the searing hot winds of May and June found the cool breeze of October somewhat chilling. And autumn produced odd indecisions. Men could not make up their minds whether or not to take extra covering for the night. Women could not decide whether or not it was time to get out their quilts and have the cotton recarded. Reluctantly they pulled out their winter bedding and brought over the carder. They felt easier when that task was done because then they could stretch and sleep soundly through hail or snow. The men were fussier; they felt the cold more; their complexion changed with the weather.

Mangal was about to turn homewards when a voice from a nearby roof hailed him. *'Oi* **Mangla!'**

Mangal looked up. He saw the moon and Salamat. 'Wait for me,' she said, 'I have some business with you.'

Mangal stopped where he was; he could hear his own heartbeat. Salamat came down a wooden ladder placed to facilitate taking up the chillies to the roof to be dried. Salamat stopped a few paces away from Mangal.

'What do you want?' asked Mangal.

'Nothing,' replied Salamat. Her voice was full of complaint. It seemed as if she wanted to cry.

'Why don't you tell me?' pleaded Mangal, stepping closer to her.

Salamat stepped back as if frightened. 'Don't come near me,' she said.

A whiff of scent came from Salamat's clothes. Mangal was familiar with the smells of the village; this smell was unfamiliar; it belonged to the cities where lust needed props such as these. It was the decadent and impersonal smell of perfume. The flame of desire lit by the autumnal evening was fanned to a fire by Salamat's words. Mangal threw caution to the winds, stepped up to the girl and asked, 'Are you afraid of me?'

'Yes,' replied Salamat. 'Have you already forgotten that day?'

'No, I have not forgotten. Only one thing remained undone.' He came a step nearer. Salamat stepped back. 'No, no, no,' she repeated till her back was against the wall. She had sworn to herself that if Mangal tried to molest her she would raise a hue and cry and have Mangal beaten up. Then she realized that if the man leapt on her and took her in a bear-hug, crushed her against his hairy chest and sealed her mouth with his lips she would not be able to scream. And the bear was advancing towards her, slowly but surely. Salamat's voice stuck in her throat; she trembled with fear. Mangal was like a man possessed . . . in one leap he would be on her. There was nothing that she could do. The two sought each other's eyes in the dark; they miauled like two tomcats. In such situations a woman usually retains her wits more than a man. But in this case it seemed as if the man had his wits about him and it was the woman who was paralysed. Then with a supreme effort Salamat twined her arms round Mangal's waist and saved herself from being taken in his embrace. Mangal asked her in a whisper: 'What do you want? Tell me.'

'Nothing! I simply thought if I met you again I'd say, "Darling, take my spinning wheel to where you plough your land."' Salamat giggled. Mangal's hands went wandering about her body. 'Are you mad?' she hissed. 'This is no time or place for . . . .'

'No?'

'No.'

'When? . . . Where can we?'

Salamat pointed to the sugar-cane field. 'There . . . when the temple bells ring and the mullah calls for prayer from the mosque.'

Mangal looked at the sugar-cane field and then up at the sky; it was covered with a thin cloud shaped like partridge feathers. 'All right,' he said.

Mangal knew that Hazari had taken out a pitcher of fermented cane juice and there was likely to be a little open space in the cane field—large enough for two people to lie on. Mangal held his peace. He realized he was letting a bird in the hand pass out of his grasp. He did not feel bold enough to force matters; perhaps a swig of liquor would put a little punch in him. He also felt unclean. The day's sweat and dust were still caked on his body. Even his mouth felt unclean; which was not surprising, considering all the incestuous abuse he had hurled at everyone. Mangal's thoughts were at variance with his words. 'All right, Salamat, don't forget,' he said absent-mindedly.

'I won't forget. You are the one who forgets,' replied Salamat.

'I will not—not this time.'

Mangal turned back. Salamat's eyes sparkling in the moonlight had fired his imagination. His step was lighter, jauntier. His spine had become as straight as a reed; from the rear he looked more like a stately pine tree than an ordinary mortal.

Salamat watched his retreating figure. The autumn had touched her fancy. The embers of passion, suddenly aflame, were as suddenly extinguished. She was no longer sure if at her midnight tryst she would be able to carry out her plan to start screaming and have Mangal apprehended. She tightened her *tehmat* about her waist and turned back homewards. On her way she met her elder sister, Inayat. 'Apa, where have you been?' asked Salamat before the other could question her.

'I went to fetch powder from Surma, the midwife.'

'Powder? What for?'

'To kill myself,' replied Inayat.

Salamat was nonplussed. Inayat blushed as she said: 'It is a shame to be born a woman.'

'*Hai*!' cried Salamat as she realized what her sister was saying. 'And the last one is not a year old yet.'

'That's why I want to kill myself.' Inayat smacked her forehead with the packet of powder. The sisters proceeded homewards. Salamat turned to her and asked, 'Have you consulted Murad on the subject?'

Murad was Inayat's husband.

'Certainly not,' replied Inayat, taking her arm. 'If I were to have children on his advice, I'd have had eleven by now. I have a belly, not an oven to bake chapattis in, have I?'

Salamat felt a little uneasy; she did not know much about these things. She believed that nature in its own inscrutable way allowed women who so wanted, to conceive and those who did not, to remain non-pregnant. 'If you go to a man this is the worst that can happen, isn't it? ... just this thing ....'

They got to their doorstep. Inayat noticed her husband flirting with her younger sister, Ayesha. She turned round and asked Salamat loudly: 'Dear, did you meet that Bhatia boy again?'

'Which one?' asked Salamat. She knew Inayat's mind was on other things.

'You know the one I mean. That ekka-driver, Mangloo.'

Salamat had time to think. The girls joined their sister, Murad and the baby. Their mother had gone out to get green chick-peas to put in the meat. No one knew where their father was. Salamat stretched herself on the charpoy and began to day-dream. She saw her shirt and *tehmat* hanging on a nail on the wall; they reminded her of her earlier disgrace. She turned red with anger. 'What on earth came over me? No one ever behaves the way I did.... If he had ordered me to take off whatsoever remained on my person, I would have taken that off too.... Sheer madness! I had to put on my shirt in the lane to cover my bosom... *Hai* Allah!... If anyone had seen me!'

Salamat worked herself into a rage... 'You've had your outing, now you can go home... that's what he said. No woman could have been insulted in this manner. What Apa thinks a disgrace doesn't bother me at all.'

Salamat busied herself serving food to the family. When the others were busy she found an opportunity to be alone with Inayat and told her of her recent meeting with Mangal. She also told her of their proposed rendezvous in the sugar-cane field near the school.

Murad went round and collected some of the toughs of the village. They were poor Arains, but they would not suffer an infidel violating the virtue of one of their womenfolk. They held a hurried consultation, got whatever weapons they could lay their hands on—staves, spears, hatchets—and went to the sugar-cane field. While they waited they talked of earlier murders in the village ... of the little girl who had been raped and of her ravisher, Tiloka.

*

Mangal had a bath and rubbed mustard oil into his beard. (He was the first in the morning at Khair Din's oil-press, to make sure he got the first drops that oozed out.) He whiled away the hours playing with Chummoo, teasing Waddi and discussing with old Jindan the problem of finding Waddi an educated babu for a husband. The house was full of laughter.

There was something fetching about Rano. She looked as if she could not have been married more than a couple of years and the children were of an older wife; or as if Mangal was the elder brother and had taken his younger brother's widow under his mantle. (How could that be? Only a younger brother was entitled to take the elder's widow! The elder brother was expected to look upon his younger brother's widow as if she were his daughter.)

Mangal never bathed in the evening. His bathing and getting into clean clothes put ideas into Rano's head. Was he doing this for her? The day had been hers; perhaps the night would also be hers ... perhaps.

Mangal looked at Rano again. Were his eyes deceiving him? Surely not! Everything about the woman—her eyes, her bosom, her cheeks, lips, thighs—just everything, seemed wanton. That morning he had seen her come out of the village pond with her wet clothes clinging to her body. She had looked like a water nymph. She had spent hours rubbing her body with a stick of turmeric till her skin had become as soft as silk. She had put a red spot on her forehead. She had stained her lips with walnut bark, and now, instead of being shrivelled up like dried raisins, they looked like a cluster of raspberries. Mangal gave her another studied look and asked, 'Did you go to the market today?'

Rano turned her large eyes on him. She saw the look in his eyes and blushed like a bride. She mumbled gently, 'Yes,' then pretended to get busy with her work. In her mind she began to plan ways of being alone with him.

What was Rano up to? It was not as if she was a woman of experience who did not want to give all she had in one throw. There was something more to the shampooing of her body, the red spot on the forehead and the staining of the lips with walnut. It was something more than making the body desirable; something more than the feminine instinct of self-preservation. Mangal was sure it was more than all that; it was something a woman only becomes aware of when that something takes complete possession of her. It was like the moon in the first quarter, which keeps most of itself hidden in darkness and on every night that follows dons a little more till it can burst out in all its silvery splendour on the fourteenth night.

How could Mangal, the ekka-driver, obsessed

with thoughts of the Arain woman, Salamat, understand the secret of the moon growing to its fullness? He had never gazed long enough at the skies. He did not realize that he was himself like the sun which dazzles those who look at it and makes them blind.

That evening, it seemed as if Rano had something special to say to Mangal—as if she wanted to unravel the bonds that tied them together and of whose existence Mangal was ignorant.

The lifted veil blinds those who have eyes—
Lift up thy veil, pretty maiden!
Hide not the pearls that are thine.
Burn not the blossoms in the fire.

Rano was determined to tear away the evil of illusion that separated her from her man and from her god. And she was determined to tear it away that night.

It seemed that Mangal also wanted to make up to her. From his shirt pocket he took out a packet of hairslides which he had bought for her on his way back from Daska. A shiver of a thrill passed down Rano's spine as she took the slides in her hand. 'Ah!' she exclaimed in an outburst of ecstasy—but only when Mangal was not listening. Mangal brought out a wad of notes and placed them in Rano's palm. Tears brimmed in Rano's eyes. She did not restrain her surprise. 'Eight rupees! How did you come by eight rupees today?'

'I got a passenger for Pasrur.'

'And?'

'And nothing. Spend them. They are all for you.' For the first time since his marriage he turned a meaningful glance on the make-up his wife had used. 'Expenses seem to have gone up too.'

For the first time since her marriage, Rano blushed like a bride. She felt that all her make-up—the turmeric stick, the henna, the walnut bark on her ruddy lips—had laid her bare. She shrank back coyly, as if covering her nakedness with a sheet. It was a curious paradox that when she wanted to get close to Mangal she did her best to get away as far as possible; and when she wanted to keep her distance from him, she became nearer. However, the night was young, the temple bells had not clanged, nor had the muezzin called for prayer.

'Give me something to eat,' demanded Mangal.

'Not yet.'

'Why not?'

Rano did not know what to say. Mangal helped her out of her dilemma: 'Have you made something nice?'

'*Aho*,' she replied. She could not contain herself. 'I've cooked a lentil soup of green chick-peas and a really spicy mint sauce to go with it.'

What a blunder! Mangal remembered his tryst. He stood up. His nostrils dilated. His hair streamed out from under his turban. He was confused; his mind was full of cobwebs. He spoke with temper: 'Give me something—anything that is ready; or I'll have to do without it. I am in a hurry.'

Rano's spirits fell. In her dream world she had cooked a different kind of meal for that night. Maybe he did have some honest business to attend to. Perhaps it would be better, because by the time he came back the children would be asleep, old Hazoor Singh would have finished with the spasms of coughing that attacked him as soon as he retired to bed, and Jindan would have got over her snoring and be slumbering more soundly . . . perhaps. It would be blissfully still and they might have to hold their breath. Mangal interrupted her train of thought: 'Where's that shirt of mine?'

Rano realized what Mangal was up to. Her hackles rose. 'Where are you going? Can't you see the sky is overcast and the breeze smells of rain!'

'I don't give a damn . . . and what business is it of yours?'

Rano's temper subsided. 'No, I have no right to ask . . . I was simply curious.'

It was different with Tiloka. In a similar situation she would have been as stubborn as a mule. 'If it isn't my business, whose business is it to stop you?' she would have demanded. She could not take that line with Mangal. She knew the 'rights' that the old, dirty and tattered sheet had conferred on her. Rano's dispirited protest had its effect on Mangal. He snapped, 'If you want to know the truth, I am going a-whoring.'

It was the sort of thing usually said by a man when he is actually going to a whore—and usually accepted by a woman as an irritable but innocent rejoinder to her inquisitiveness. Or why should a man admit he is going to fornicate? But Rano had been through life's mill and had greater intuition than most women. The Goddess had made of her a full-grown woman with feminine wiles and one who was therefore aware of men and the fact that they often succumb to every passing temptation. Perhaps that is the reason why the Creator has made men's bodies such complicated networks of nerves and arteries.

The request for the shirt confirmed Rano's worst suspicions. She stood up, stubborn as a mule. Her nostrils dilated with anger. The woman in her had entered the arena to fight for the rights of a wife—and if necessary she was willing to descend to the level of a prostitute and use all the weapons in her armoury. Rano knew her adversary—the full-bosomed and firm-bodied Salamat—the Salamat who did not need walnut bark to stain her lips, nor a red spot on her forehead to make her desirable. The man was like a rock of granite or a bar of steel and lusted after a woman as hard as the elements he was made of. All this Rano comprehended and was prepared to countenance. She flung a meaningful glance at the tin trunk and said, 'It's in there . . . your shirt.'

From the lane outside somebody called, 'Rano!' It was her friend, Vidya.

Rano ran to the door. Before Vidya could speak, Rano pushed her away. 'Not now, Vidya; please go away.'

Vidya stood her ground. 'Why? What is the matter?'

Rano joined the palms of her hands in prayer. 'For God's sake, for the sake of your ancestors . . . go!'

Vidya turned away, but looked over her shoulder many times as she went.

*

When Rano came back, Mangal had the trunk open. His clothes were lying scattered on the floor. He had a bottle of orange liquor in his hand. His eyes were sparkling. 'Where did this come from?' he demanded.

'What?'

'This thing?' repeated Mangal, holding aloft the bottle. 'The bottle of orange liquor?'

Rano glanced nervously at the door and replied, 'How should I know?'

Dabboo came to her help; he began to howl. Rano peered out of the door, waved her arm at the dog and cried, 'Death come to you! Why are you wailing in your own courtyard? Go and howl somewhere where they cook vegetables and meat.' She turned back to Mangal. 'Your brother used to drink the stuff.'

'Yes, I know, but . . . after all these years,' he said with surprise.

'It must have lain there all the time. I have not touched the trunk since he went.'

Mangal turned the bottle in his hand and examined its contents with unbelieving eyes. This was exactly what he had been looking for all evening—the stuff that would bolster up his courage, give him the agile nimbleness of a roebuck and a ten-horsepower punch in his groin .... He had visions of the sturdy, lusty village wench awaiting him in the sugar-cane field. He came to the threshold and looked up at the sky. The clouds had gathered the moon in their dark folds.

Somewhere the summer had prolonged its lease; somewhere dust-storms had blown. What other reason could there be for clouds over Kotla in autumn! Or was it the summer solstice? Mangal saw a few stars peering through the blanket of clouds and satisfied himself that the night was young. But it was a different Mangal—a callous, indifferent Mangal.

'I have a swig or two at times at the Naseebanwala tonga-stand.' He emphasized his words by sticking the thumb of his left hand into his mouth.

'I know,' replied Rano.

Mangal did not express surprise; he did not care whether or not Rano knew. He looked briefly at the bottle. Tears brimmed in Rano's eyes; her breath became heavier and more menacing.

'I will not drink in your presence,' he said in the same nonchalant tone.

'Why not?' demanded Rano, fully on her guard.

'Because I know you do not like it.'

The words were on her lips, 'Why should I mind? What right have I to object?' But an inner voice spoke the truth and the hatred in her eyes emphasized her feelings: 'I loathe it like poison.'

Rano had guessed correctly. She knew her man well, she wanted him to react in a particular way; and he did. Mangal twisted the cork of the bottle in his mouth and spoke in a tone of mock bravado: 'This is the worst trait of married women—nagging their men about what they should eat or drink.' Suddenly he felt he had said too much.

Rano felt pleased that in talk at least she had been able to establish a man-woman relationship with Mangal. Nevertheless she kept up the pretence of being annoyed: 'Don't you dare drink this stuff! I won't ever let you . . . . '

And just as Rano had foreseen, Mangal wrenched off the cork and spat it to the ground. The stench of alcohol flooded the room. Rano drew her dupatta across her nose and put her hand over the mouth of the bottle. Mangal grabbed her by the arm and hissed in her ear, 'I'll drink what I like, and I like this stuff.'

'You were the one to stop your brother from taking it; you were the one to break the bottle; and you were the one to rescue me from his clutches . . . . Do you remember?'

'I was sorry for you—nothing more.'

As Rano had foreseen, Mangal began to force her to release her grip on the bottle. Waddi came in, saw them close to each other, and stopped abruptly. A flash of lightning lit up the courtyard and the three figures in the dark room. Then came the clap of thunder.

'Go and feed the children and put them to bed in the other room,' said Rano to Waddi. 'It looks as if it will rain.'

Waddi went out and shut the door behind her. She had noticed the change in her mother's behaviour since the morning and had a vague inkling of what was brewing.

Rano renewed her struggle to take away the bottle. Mangal tried to push her away—and when she persisted, smacked her on the face, bosom and behind with his large, calloused hands. Whenever he was able to shake her off, he put the bottle to his mouth, took a swig, and swore, 'I am not an impotent nobody like my brother; I won't give in to a woman so easily.'

Mangal put down a third of the liquor in the bottle while fighting with Rano. Rano made a final, desperate bid to wrench the bottle out of his hands. Mangal pushed her to the floor, sat heavily on her belly and slapped her on the face many times—exactly as Rano had foreseen.

The more Rano struggled to get up, the more violently Mangal pushed her down. And with one hand free he tilted the remains of the bottle into his mouth. His face turned red; the blood mounted to his ears and head. Rano's bosom swelled like a pair of bellows. The animation in her body became too much for Mangal. Rano made yet another attempt to free herself; Mangal smashed her skull against the wall.

A trickle of blood oozed from Rano's head. She felt weak and gave up the struggle. She lay flat on her back with her eyes closed and her mouth wide open. The silence that followed reached old Jindan's ears. 'What is the matter, Rano?' came the enquiry.

'It's nothing, Aunty! Only a cat,' replied Rano in a delicious swoon. She felt the life ebb out of her limbs. Her hands lay where they were; her legs spread out, her clothes in disarray. She could not tell whether it was the orange liquor or water which made her salwar damp. It was hard to tell which of the two had imbibed the liquor, Rano or Mangal, and which one was sober and which drunk.

Mangal stood up and gazed at the woman lying at his feet. 'Strange woman!' he thought. 'After all the thrashing, she says it was a cat.' He felt ashamed of himself and grateful to Rano.

Mangal tore off an end of his turban to staunch the blood flowing from Rano's head. He warmed the rag with his breath and pressed it gently on her bruises—just as Rano had done for him many nights earlier. It was a pleasant sensation. Mangal felt he was atoning for his misdeeds. He clutched at Rano's feet. Rano pulled him over her body and held him close to her—as if it was she who had to make up to Mangal for having beaten him.

'Do forgive me! You must!' blabbered Mangal like a child.

'Swear you will not drink again!' said Rano, holding him tighter. Her feminine instinct warned her of the danger of going too far. 'If you give me your word, I will give you a drink with my own hands.'

'I swear,' replied Mangal, without being clear in his mind about what he was forswearing.

Rano slipped out quietly. Mangal waited, listening to the musical pitter-patter of the rain falling on the kitchen utensils. Waddi had served the evening meal and put the children to bed. It seemed that gods and mortals had conspired to bring about the consummation of the affair. Rano covered the oven with a wicker basket and brought a trayful of food and another bottle of orange liquor for Mangal. There were chapattis on one side, meat chops and a freshly sliced onion on the other. Mangal looked from the meat chops to Rano. He began to drool at the mouth. Rano poured the orange liquor in a tumbler and held it out to him. Mangal could not believe his eyes. He gazed into Rano's eyes. He could not refuse. He took the tumbler from her hands. 'If I drink after today, let there be no food for me,' he said, as he raised the tumbler to his lips.

'Wait!' commanded Rano. She had remembered something. She ran out into the rain. She came back with a saucer on which were eight slices of tomato, thinly cut into heart shapes.

Mangal fell upon the food and drink. It was better than anything he got at the tonga-stand. With trembling hands Rano continued to fill the tumbler with orange liquor. And it was Rano who began to feel inebriated, expansive and carefree. Her dupatta slipped from her head and fell to the ground. The buttons of her chemise came undone.

The temple bells began to clang; the muezzin gave the call for prayer.

'O hell!' swore Mangal when he heard the pealing of the bells and the sonorous call of the mullah.

'Hell what?' asked Rano.

Mangal pointed towards the house of Jhelum Arain and explained. 'To hell with all these Hindu pandits and Muslim mullahs.'

Mangal made a half-hearted attempt to keep his appointment. He went to the end of the courtyard, saw how dark it was and reeled back to his room. He peered as hard as he could and caught sight of Rano standing motionless right in front of him . . . like the full moon in all its glory.

'Why . . . why?' asked Mangal, lisping. 'Why have you got your clothes on you?'

Rano picked up her net dupatta and stretched it out between her and Mangal. 'Here, I've taken them off.' Her clothes peeled off her body. Only the gossamer-thin gauze of the dupatta intervened. A third dimension of feminine beauty was revealed to Mangal. And what man who had suckled his mother's breast can deny the elemental compulsion of the female form? The floods of passion burst through the flimsy dam that had held them in check. Then the fifty-two weeks of the year, seven days of the week, twenty-four hours of the day and night—hours, minutes, seconds—all conceptions of time were telescoped into a timeless eternity. It was one of those memorable occasions when the moon takes the sun in its embrace and in the lunar eclipse draws all its heat from crown to toe. Mangal groped like a blind man; his flailing arms grabbed Rano. In a trice the two were enveloped in a burning passion as fiery as a field of saffron. 'Brother's wife, how lovely you look tonight,' breathed Mangal in

Rano's ear. He continued repeating the words till his breath came shorter and shorter and he went over the edge of the precipice into an orgasmic chasm.

*

Salamat stood at her threshold scowling at the drizzle. She slapped her own face and then her thighs and hissed as if she had swallowed a mouthful of red-hot chillies. The clang of the temple bells faded into silence. The mullah's call for prayer became a distant echo in her ear. Salamat also cursed the men of religion who, although they had nothing to do with the making of a human body, did not restrain themselves from denying its compulsions and censuring its conduct.

It was nearing midnight. It rained intermittently. In the veranda of the school beside the sugar-cane field, the men waited for Mangal. Murad looked up at the clouds and said irritably, 'Friends, I think this woman Salamat is a windbag.'

Khalifa grunted in agreement. Allah Dad and Hakuman nodded their heads. They picked up their staves, spears and hatchets and went out into the downpour. 'He's saved his skin, that bloody Sikhra,' they said as they wended their way homewards.

Salamat saw her brother-in-law, Murad, come home without fulfilling his murderous mission. She stretched herself on the charpoy. 'Allah be thanked!' she exclaimed as she yawned and fell asleep.

Six

The sun was hidden behind the scattered clouds. A poor peasant fatigued by the labours of the preceding night had covered himself with his tattered sheet and was sleeping the sleep of the just.

A strong breeze blew from beyond the hills. It brought with it flocks of migratory birds from distant lands—from the Siberian marshes, the mountains of the Caucasus, the plateaux of the Pamirs and the peaks of the Sulaiman range. It seemed as if innumerable miles away, children had floated millions of paper boats on the stream of time—or perhaps Goddess Amba or Vaishno Devi had flung into it the hoard of sugar *patashas* left by generations of pilgrims who had come to pay her homage.

So passed the summer solstice. The nights grew longer; the days, shorter. The sun peered coyly through the folds of the clouds; its beams spread like a warm smile over the cold, damp earth. The grey clouds were touched with pink.

The peasants espied the wanton heaving of the dew-washed bosom of mother earth. It was more than they could resist. They got down to tilling the soil and sowing new seed. The village lads broke off the branches of the mulberry tree, made bows and shot their wavering darts with aimless abandon. The pandit of the temple and the mullah of the mosque prepared for the sacrifice.

Mangal got out the harness of the ekka and fixed the plume. Rano uncovered the oven. To get rid of the damp, she filled the oven with firewood and set it alight. Of the eight rupees Mangal had given her the evening before, she gave Waddi one to buy fresh ghee from a neighbouring household. The twins were at school taking their half-yearly tests. She sent the youngest, Chummoo, to get radishes and potatoes from the house of Jhelum Arain. Chummoo saw Salamat with her hair in curlers. Salamat noticed Chummoo just as he was tying the radishes and potatoes in a bundle. She asked: 'What's on, Chummoo? Are you having chapattis of radish and potatoes?'

'Not chapattis,' replied Chummoo haughtily, 'parathas! Ma has heated the oven.'

'*Oho!*' exclaimed Jhelum intervening. 'So your mother's fired her oven, has she now?'

'Sure!' answered Chummoo, vigorously wagging his head. 'If you want to bake parathas, you are welcome. Or you can send Salamat instead.'

The boy took the vegetables and went home. Jhelum, Inayat and Ayesha burst into fits of laughter. Salamat complained of an acid stomach.

The aroma of parathas cooking spread over the courtyard, teasing the appetites of Hazoor Singh and Jindan. Hazoor Singh could not contain himself. 'Daughter, bake a few soft ones for me. My teeth aren't what they used to be.' This incited Jindan to retort, 'Just look at the old man! He cannot think of anything but food.'

Rano made a bundle of warm parathas and handed it to Mangal. Mangal gazed at her with his besotted eyes and nodded towards the others in the courtyard. 'You have a lot of work to do.'

'I know,' replied Rano, looking down. She raised her head and continued, 'What else were we women created for except work?'

Mangal was ready to leave when Rano remembered she had something to say to him. 'Wait,' she shouted.

Mangal stopped where he was. Rano came close to him. Without her voice faltering, she asked, 'Get me material for two salwars. I need something for the festival.'

Before Mangal could answer, Rano pointed to her bosom. 'All women wear something here; I only have my kameez.' She bared her pearly teeth and laughed. Mangal smiled. 'I'll see what I can do about it,' he replied.

'What do you mean, "I'll see what I can do about it?" You'll have to do something about it,' insisted Rano. 'Do you want me to go about without a salwar? I won't lose anything.'

Mangal shook his head, as if he did not want to share that privilege with any stranger. Rano pursed her lips and continued, 'Channo's husband got her a piece of black silk. Black is most becoming on her fair skin.'

Rano caught the hem of Mangal's shirt. 'Try to get more passengers for Pasrur; if not Pasrur, Kinghranwaley, Sialkot or Sabhrial. The boys could do with new shorts too.'

Mangal was inundated with these sweet-and-sour requests. The plume fell from the harness. Mangal picked it up and began to refix it. Rano still held on to the hem of his shirt—almost as if she had a lien on him, as if he was indebted to her.

'All right, *baba*! All right!' exclaimed Mangal as he turned away. Rano stood on her threshold idly watching his retreating figure, the figure of her man. One night had fulfilled the promise of many days and many months. Rano shivered. 'No, no, it was not Tiloka, it was Mangal.'

But it was not the same Mangal she had seen the day Channo had mentioned the possibility of her marrying him. Now he was silent, struck dumb and weighed down under the obligations of love. No wonder he looked so much like his elder brother! Rano turned back, after she had taken the full imprint of Mangal's figure upon her mind. That morning there was more self-assurance in her gait. Everything seemed lighter and gayer. She got down to plastering her courtyard with fresh mud, to make it more suitable for receiving visitors.

No one had expected such an influx of pilgrims at Kotla. Nor had anyone known it to snow so early on the mountains. The pilgrims had to wait at Kotla. Goddess Amba had ordained that her devotees should sojourn in the village; that there should be an assemblage of pilgrims from Pasrur, Gujranwala, Sabhrial, Sialkot, Sattoki and Satrah. Some came by bus; some in bullock-carts; some on ekkas.

No one could have foretold the windfall that would fill the homes of Kotla's peasants with plenty. Diwan Shah, the grocer, sold all his groceries; the peasants sold their stocks of ghee; Khair Din got rid of all his oil, and Jhelum her vegetables. Even the temple pigeons had their fill. They flew down from the steeple to feed in the village lanes; they billed and cooed like the *kooh, kooh* of the flour-mill. The village guest-house, the serai and the zaildar's house were crammed. The visitors paid up to Rs. 20 for a hovel. The goldsmiths palmed off their stocks of ear-rings; the silversmiths palmed off their plates; the potters, their earthen vessels and lamps. Even the poor banyan tree was stripped of its leaves and the arch above the pulpit in the mosque was robbed of its hive of honey. The stream of pilgrims continued to flow in. They came in parties, dancing and singing:

'Save us sinners, Goddess Amba!
The time of redemption is at hand.'

No one could explain why at this time of the year the girls of Kotla became gentle in their manners but tougher inside. Some explained the change as due to the heat of the summer that had gone by; others, by the winter to come. All of them found in it a subject for speculation and jest. This left the girls undisturbed. Every morning they went out in their droves to the temple. They carried brass platters full of flowers and *sindhur* powder. It was wonderful to see their swaying hips as they went. Occasionally, one would stop for a while and lean against the flame-tree. The gesture was enough to send the pulses of the village swains into a wild flutter. As soon as the girls were beyond hearing, the boys would exult: '*Hoi, hoi!*'

It was the biggest festival of the year. Even Hazoor Singh and Jindan went to the temple. But Waddi, who had never failed to make her obeisance to the Goddess, stayed at home with her mother—it was not safe for a girl of her age to mingle in the milling crowds of lusty youths. Rano was grinding some kind of red paste in her pestle and mortar and putting it in a copper cup. A green chilli showed its head above the batter of gram flour. Slices of potatoes were ready for the pan of boiling mustard oil.

Channo came in, dressed in black silk. She flaunted a pink dupatta on her head. She had a low-cut blouse which revealed her fair skin. When she saw Rano in the kitchen, she cried, 'Fie on you, woman! At home on a day like this! Are you a corpse or something?'

Rano simply shook her head.

Channo came closer and whispered in her ear,

'All the girls are out there, waiting to have a go at you. Why are you glued to the kitchen?' Channo noticed the floral pattern of Rano's salwar. 'So that's what it is!' she exclaimed touching the salwar.

Rano quickly immersed the long-handled sieve in the oil. Channo's eyes fell on the low cut of Rano's blouse. She thrust her hand down Rano's bosom and withdrew it with a jerk as if she had touched a live ember. '*Hai, hai*, death come to me! It seems that at long last Mangal has done his job!'

It was a loaded remark. Rano did not deign to reply. She put a bit of the red and green paste she had been grinding on her tongue and began to smack her lips.

'What's this?' demanded Channo. She looked more closely and saw that it was sweet-sour chutney. She took a little on her finger and put it to her mouth. It burnt her and made her cry '*Si, si*!'. She grabbed Rano by the shoulder and shook her. 'What have you been up to, you whore of a widow?'

'Up to? What?' queried Rano, pretending she did not understand.

'Out with the truth,' ordered Channo, 'or you'll see me dead! I put you on oath!'

Rano scowled and nodded towards Waddi. She drew Channo close to her and whispered one word into her ear: 'Yes.'

A shiver went down Channo's spine. She put one hand on her head, the other on her waist and performed a pirouette. She ran out shouting at the top of her voice. '*Nee* Pooro, *nee* Vidya! Sarupo *nee* . . . . Girls, where have you all disappeared to!'

Channo was too excited to see where she was going. On the threshold she had a head-on collision with Mangal. Channo reeled back and hit the wall. Mangal's turban came off, his top-knot was loosened and his long hair became scattered over his face. He was a funny sight.

Channo feigned anger and scolded, 'Are you blind! Can't you see where you are going?'

'But . . . but Channo . . .' spluttered Mangal. Before he could say any more Channo ran out. Mangal picked up his turban and dusted his clothes. He called, 'Rano!'

This was the first time that Mangal had called her by her name. Once more Rano was full of expectations. Mangal sat down on his haunches close to her—as if he had a secret to impart. 'Listen Rano . . . a strange thing happened . . . quite incredible.'

Rano could have shouted for joy. But she kept a straight, solemn face and said in a nonchalant tone, 'After you have told me your story, I will also tell you mine.'

'What?'

'Your turn first.'

Mangal noticed Waddi standing by the wall. The girl was looking away, but her ears were obviously tuned in to hear what was passing between her stepfather and mother. Mangal addressed her with great tenderness, 'Daughter, will you go in for a moment?'

Waddi went indoors as meek as a little child. Mangal continued: 'Amongst the pilgrims is a lad of about 25 . . . strong as a lion . . . . He is the son of a petition-writer at Daska . . . they have lands, houses, shops—all kinds of property.'

Rano's face fell. 'If they are rich, they will demand something.'

'Let me finish my tale,' interrupted Mangal impatiently. 'He says if he marries anyone, it will be Waddi . . . no other girl in the world but Waddi.'

'Not really!' exclaimed Rano full of disbelief. She stopped work.

'I swear,' assured Mangal.

Rano became excited. Her breath came faster; her legs shook. She restrained her emotions and asked: 'Has he seen Waddi?'

'He must have—not that it matters.'

'Of course it does! If he has not seen her or met her, why should he want to marry her?'

'I don't know. But the elders of the village are all for it. And you know what they say, the voice of the five elders is the voice of God: *Panchon mein Parmeshwar.*'

'That's true,' conceded Rano. 'If that wasn't true, where would I be today?'

After a while Mangal continued, 'They say your daughter is destined to have a great future. She'll be a queen. She'll be a real queen—not like you, Rano. You are only one in name.'

The words flowed over Rano's head; she heard his voice, but not what he was saying. Mangal went on in his monotone, 'He does not want any dowry; on the contrary, even the mention of the word makes him angry.' It crossed Mangal's mind that

Rano might misunderstand him, so he quickly added, 'That does not mean I won't give her anything; of course I will give whatever is customary. No, I will not let down my daughter.'

Rano could hardly believe her ears. 'My daughter'—that was what he had said.

'I would sell myself into slavery for her sake,' continued Mangal. 'I would even mortgage my ekka and pony.' He recalled Rano had also something to tell him. 'Wasn't there something you wanted to tell me?'

'It wasn't anything important,' replied Rano. 'When you go out next, bring Surma the midwife. I must fix things with her.'

'The midwife!' repeated Mangal. His eyes widened with eagerness as he asked, 'Is it really true?'

Rano smiled; she shook her head slightly and looked away in embarrassment. Suddenly the courtyard was invaded by a host of women singing and dancing. They were Channo, Pooran Dei, Vidya, Janki, Sarupo, Chandi and a host of others.

'You showed your arm full of bracelets
And gained a handsome lover;
With two-pice worth of paint on your lips
You gained a handsome lover.'

Mangal raised his hands to silence them. 'Channo... Aunty,' he tried. Pooran Dei stepped in front and gave Mangal a violent push. 'Off with you, you're getting too big for your boots.'

'He thinks no end of himself now,' added Channo giving him another push.

'Get out from here—a buck in a herd of does! You've no business here!' said Vidya.

'Shameless creature!' swore Pooran Dei. 'You've done your job. Now go and ply your ekka.' She turned to Rano, 'You'd better bear a son or there'll be no end to your troubles.'

The women began to belabour Mangal and push him out. Rano tried to intervene. She laughed, but she also had tears in her eyes. '*Hai*, lay off my man! That's enough; or do you want to kill him?' Mangal covered his face and head with his hands and edged backwards towards the door. 'Aunty Channo! . . . All right, all right, I'll go. Let me alone. Heaven help me!' he shouted as he got out of the door.

The women had the field to themselves. The singing and dancing were resumed with greater gusto. One sang the *tappa*.

'Get the cauldron on the boil—it's a boy!'

The chorus replied:

'A lovely saucy boy — ho!
A smart, spicy boy — ho!
Get the cauldron on the boil—it's a boy!'

They got crazier as they whirled round faster and faster. The din was deafening. Rano took Pooran Dei aside and shouted in her ear,

'Congratulations, Aunty!'

'Congratulations? What on earth for?' asked Pooran Dei, tightening her dhoti about her waist.

'We've found a husband for Waddi.'

The minds of village women are obsessed with weddings, with grooms on horseback and brides in veils. Their ears ever await the shehnai playing marriage airs, and they look forward to bridegrooms' parties. The news of Waddi's betrothal was greeted with wild enthusiasm. They could see the wedding before their eyes. They did not bother to ask, 'Who is the boy? Where is he from? What does he do?' They only saw a groom on horseback, his face covered with tinsel, a royal aigrette on his turban and a sword in his hand. They sang:

'Two lemons ripe beneath the creeper
My husband's elder brother wants to borrow them.'
'Brother-in-law, I don't sell my lemon
And I don't lend my lemons.
My branches are weighed down with lemons
They dangle like rings in the ears.'

Someone took up the refrain of another song:

'O father-in-law, you are dark brown as an almond;
Your sons' wives are fair, but your sons are black.'

In their world of fancy, the women had sent all the brides of the world to their husbands' homes.

The noise and merry-making diverted many

people bound for the temple to Mangal's home; it seemed as if the Goddess had changed her abode from the temple to this house.

The village sarpanch, headman Tara Singh, Kesar Singh, Ruldoo, Diwana, Dulla, Karmoo—the whole lot—came into the courtyard. The rooftops were crowded with women; the lanes with men. Surma was also there—Surma who had assisted at the birth of all Kotla's children and would undoubtedly help with the birth of generations to come.

Jhelum's three daughters, Inayat, Ayesha and Salamat, trooped in. Nawab's wife, Ayesha, and Gurdas's wife Gunawanti, who had never got on with each other, forgot their past quarrels and joined in the merry-making. Pooran Dei and Vidya forced Rano to join them.

Then there was the dog, Dabboo, running around in circles, sniffing people's bottoms and wagging a friendly tail at strangers.

The years of misery had taken their toll of Rano's looks. Few people had noticed that beneath the pall of sorrow was a woman of remarkable beauty. Now that her worries were over, Rano had come into her own. Her bosom seemed to burst from her striped shirt; her silk salwar with its little flowers shimmered like a garter-snake spiralling skywards. When she raised her hands to dance the *gidda*, it was enough to floor anyone. Rano's new beauty became the popular topic of conversation amongst the men of Kotla.

The girls danced in a whirl which made the old

and the young standing round appear a mass of faces. Then the faces became blobs of different colours; then the colours became like sunbeams which have all the colours of the world in them but require human ingenuity to be broken into a spectrum. Through the flying garments, men saw a good deal more of the girls than they had before.

Out of the village common there was another kind of festivity. An enormous mob of pilgrims had turned up and were chanting hymns in praise of the Goddess. They had come to have their sins forgiven—the sins they had committed and the sins they were going to commit in the future. They danced as they sang:

'In the court of the Queen Goddess,
The Celestial Mother,
Are lit celestial lamps.
O Mother Divine!
Seven fair sisters you are—
Flowers of coral in your hair.
In my Queen Mother's court
Is lit the eternal lamp.'

The scene became truly bizarre. Chaudhry Meharban Das and his brother, Ghanisham Das, returned home after serving their sentences in jail. They followed the noisy procession of dancing pilgrims. Their heads were bent low; their eyes, fixed on the ground. They prostrated themselves on the ground as they went. Their ears were red from being pulled in repentance. They had no words to say it, but their silence was an eloquent admission of their guilt.

Then there was a young lad between the two. He was a strapping, handsome youth of twenty-five. He sang the hymn of praise of the Goddess with great fervour and devotion. Who was he? What sin could one so young have committed that he should have to crave forgiveness in this manner?

Mangal clove his way through the jostling, buffeting crowd and got to Rano. He shook Rano by the shoulder and pointed to the youth: 'Rano, that's the fellow.'

Rano gazed at the handsome youth. Her eyes sparkled. She blessed the lad as her son-in-law to be. How broad-shouldered and how handsome he was! What mother could ask for a nicer husband for her daughter! Rano was overcome with joy. She took Channo in her arms and hugged her till Channo could not breathe. 'Channo, I have been saved; the gods have been good to me,' she exulted.

Waddi peered over the heads of the women to see the lad for herself. In the crowd she felt anonymous and unselfconscious. The blood rushed to her face. Salamat, who was standing close by, turned pale. She took her elders sister's arm and said, 'Apa, let's go home. I am very tired.'

Rano became like a little child showing off her favourite toy. 'Look Aunty Vidya! You must see him . . . and Channo, you whore, you can have a look too! Lajo, there he is . . . '

Aunty Pooran Dei had a good look at him. Vidya examined his finer points, as if he were a stallion for sale. Chandi weighed his pros and cons. Lajo, Janki and Kuki turned their critical eyes on him. And Rano heard their comments in turn and agreed enthusiastically, 'How right you are!'

*

Rano's starry-eyed gaze changed suddenly. She saw the pallor come to Channo's face. Rano shrieked, '*Hai nee*! What's the matter?' Then Rano saw for herself. The youth stood close by her. His eyes were on her lap, the palms of his hands were joined together as if he were begging for a favour. Rano screamed, 'May death come to me!'

Rano's face became as white as a sheet. Her hands shook. A cold sweat broke out over her entire body. 'He is the same fellow, the one who murdered my . . . ' Rano's head reeled. Before she fainted, old Hazoor Singh hobbled up and put his arm behind her and saved her from falling backwards.

'Daughter-in-law,' he stuttered, 'what do you have to lament? Look at me. I have given away two sons to get one real one.'

That was all the man could say. Tears rolled down his cheeks and were lost in his beard. Since the death of Tiloka, Hazoor Singh had been looking for someone who could take the place of his son. He had often told himself in his quivering voice:

> '*Yogi, why lookest thou in the dust?*
> *A ruby once lost is never found.*'

Hazoor Singh had freed himself from worldly attachments, but the new situation raised emotions which compelled his bleary eyes to respond. His was the vision, he the visionary, he the play and the action in it. His saffron turban kept loosening. When he wiped away his tears or blew his nose into the free end of his turban his face became covered with saffron and he looked like a yogi who had renounced the world. As a matter of fact, Hazoor Singh had renounced the world; it was the world which refused to renounce Hazoor Singh. Standing at death's door, an inner vision had been granted to him. In a flash he saw the meaning of life and death . . . . At the centre of the stage was Rano, the eternal daughter-in-law. Rano was the one who appeared out of nowhere in every wedding, with her wedding dupatta, her arms covered with red lacquer bracelets, folding the palms of her henna-stained hands, and pleading with her half-opened, bashful eyes: 'Father of our fathers, give me this son of yours. I will return your gift tenfold. I will give you ten sons who will look like him and be like him . . . . ' And the hoary ancestor answered: 'Your request shall be my command. But this son of mine . . . this . . . . ' The emotion was too much for old Hazoor Singh and he turned away.

Hazoor Singh ran his trembling fingers through Rano's long, black hair. Rano had found her long-lost father. She ignored convention; she bent her head against Hazoor Singh's breast and cried. 'No, no, Bapu, this can never be . . . . Not for my daughter . . . I'd rather kill myself.'

The scene attracted the pilgrims from the temple. They awaited the judgement. It seemed as if the future of the world rested on Rano's verdict. If she said 'Yes,' life would begin again. If she said 'No,' it would spell the doom of the world. And what a cataclysm that would be! Nothing would be spared—neither human beings nor animals, neither birds nor beasts, neither earth nor sky. Time would stop moving. The word would lose its voice; the torch its light. God Himself would cease to be.

The five elders of the village stood in a row in front of Rano. The simple-minded Mangal was the sixth.

Hazoor Singh patted Rano on her head and asked, 'Daughter, what is all this about? Why have events taken this turn? You do not know the answer. I do not know the answer. Not one of the people here knows the answer. Do not try to unravel this great mystery. The proper answer is silence . . . silence so complete that not even the sound of a breath can be heard.'

Rano turned round to see her daughter. Waddi looked distracted. She did not open her mouth. But it was clear to Rano that if she said 'No,' her daughter would for ever hold her responsible for her remaining a lonely spinster. Rano lifted her head from her father-in-law's shoulder and spoke distinctly, 'Bapu, it shall be as you wish.'

The crowd awaited the decision with bated breath. Some had brought gifts for the betrothal. Suddenly they began to sing and dance and yell.

Rano raised her eyes towards the temple of the Goddess. Tears of gratitude streamed down her cheeks and a beatific smile lit up her face.

The crowds dispersed. The shades of twilight deepened into night. Even in the pitch black of the darkness a bright light played about Rano's face. The temple bells began their clamour. The muezzin called the faithful to prayer. Above the steeple of the temple, Rano saw the figure of a woman. Her long hair was scattered about her shoulders. Rano raised her hands to the apparition and cried: 'Mother! Mother of mankind! Goddess Divine!'

MORE ABOUT PENGUINS

For further information about books available from Penguins in India write to Penguin Books (India) Ltd, 210 Chiranjiv Tower 43, Nehru Place, New Delhi 110 019.

In the UK: For a complete list of books available from Penguins in the United King-dom write to Dept. EP, Penguin Books Ltd, Harmondsworth, Middlesex UB7 0DA.

In the U.S.A.: For a complete list of books available from Penguins in the United States write to Dept. DG, Penguin Books, 299 Murray Hill Parkway, East Rutherford, New Jersey 07073.

In Canada: For a complete list of books available from Penguins in Canada write to Penguin Books Canada Ltd, 2801 John Street, Markham, Ontario L3R 1B4.

In Australia: For a complete list of books available from Penguins in Australia write to the Marketing Department, Penguin Books Australia Ltd, P.O. Box 257, Ringwood, Victoria 3134.

In New Zealand: For a complete list of books available from Penguins in New Zealand write to the Marketing Department, Penguin Books (N.Z.) Ltd, Private Bag, Takapuna, Auckland 9.

FOR THE BEST IN PAPERBACKS, LOOK FOR THE 🐧

DELHI : A NOVEL
Khushwant Singh

Delhi is Khushwant Singh's vast, erotic, irreverent *magnum opus* on the city. The principal narrator of the saga, which extends over six hundred years, is a bawdy, ageing reprobate who loves Delhi as much as he does the *hijda* whore, Bhagmati—half man, half woman with the sexual inventiveness and energy of both the sexes. Travelling through time, space and history to 'discover' his beloved city the narrator meets a myriad of people—poets and princes, saints and sultans, temptresses and traitors, emperors and eunuchs—who have participated in (and been witness to) the major historical forces that have shaped and endowed Delhi with its very special mystique . . . And as we accompany the narrator on his epic journey, we find the city of emperors transformed and immortalized in our minds forever.

'. . . (*Delhi* is) Khushwant Singh at his salacious best.'

—*Time*

FOR THE BEST IN PAPERBACKS, LOOK FOR THE 🐧

NOT A NICE MAN TO KNOW: THE BEST OF KHUSHWANT SINGH

Edited by Nandini Mehta

In an essay in this anthology, Khushwant Singh claims that he is not a nice man to know. Whatever the truth of this assertion, there is little question about his skill as a witty, eloquent and entertaining writer. This book collects the best of over three decades of the author's prose—including his finest journalistic pieces, short stories, translations, jokes, plays as well as excerpts from his non-fiction books and novels. Taken together, the pieces in this selection (some of them never published before) show just why Khushwant Singh is the country's most widely read columnist and one of its most celebrated authors.

'The book is a good buy...is highly readable and thoroughly enjoyable.'

—— Indian Reviews of Books

'Easily the finest Khushwant Singh companion to be published yet, the book reproduces the best of his columns, articles, translations, fiction, jokes and a play.'

—India Today

FOR THE BEST IN PAPERBACKS, LOOK FOR THE 🐧

THE HUNTED
Mudra Rakshasa

Translated from the Hindi by Robert A. Hueckstedt

Tension mounts as upper-caste landowners in the remote Uttar Pradesh village find their traditional 'lathi-or-chapatti' hold over the lower castes threatened by the arrival of Master Bhooray Lal, a schoolteacher-turned-rebel, who, along with a gang of zealous, though ragtag, recruits, seeks to fuel a revolt 'of the masses.' To keep the villagers in check the landowners resort to various punitive measures, actively aided by the local police. Bhooray Lal, infuriated, tells the villagers to fight or succumb... this time they fight.

'... A fine example of the modern Indian novel....a kind of fictionalized reportage on contemporary Indian reality.'

—*Sunday*

FOR THE BEST IN PAPERBACKS, LOOK FOR THE 🐧

A RIVER CALLED TITASH
Advaita Malla Barman
Translated by Kalpana Bardhan

On the banks of the Titash lives a vibrant community of fisherfolk, the Malos, who in their love of music and poetry, transcend their lack of material wealth. Their days are filled with laughter and rejoicing. And then the idyll ends. The fickle river shows its capacity for destruction as do powerful oppressors; between them the Malos are driven to the brink of despair....

On another level, *A River Called Titash* is also the story of Ananta, who embarks on a solitary quest for knowledge; Ananta's mother, whose fierce sense of honour eventually destroys her; and Kishore, whose restlessness makes him undertake a journey that ends in madness.

With its deftly orchestrated plot, stark realism, limpid style and elegance of structure, *A River Called Titash* is a masterpiece of contemporary Bengali literature.

FOR THE BEST IN PAPERBACKS, LOOK FOR THE 🐧

RAAG DARBARI
Shrilal Shukla
Translated from the Hindi by Gillian Wright

Life in Shivpalganj crawls at a leisurely pace, unfolding at evening bhang-drinking sessions, the village wrestling pit, in nearby lentil fields, at gambling sessions and country *melas*... M A pass Rangnath has just arrived here for some rest and relaxation. His host is his Uncle Vaidyaji, the local doctor, who pontificates on everything from ayurveda to politics to the 'essence' of life. Vaidyaji is also Shivpalganj's most important citizen... Hanging on to Vaidyaji's coat-tails are a host of oddballs, including a college principal who never wants the College Committee to meet, and Sanichar, a layabout bhang-grinder who becomes Pradhan-elect of the Village Council....

But a rebellion is brewing among the college teachers, and Vaidyaji's sworn arch-rival, Ramadhin Bhikmakhervi, Shivpalganj's gambling dada, opium dealer and poet to boot, won't give up the Village Council, his domain, without a fight ... lawsuits fly, the grain cooperative is ransacked, a Vaidyaji hoodlum ends up in the town court on a trumped-up burglary charge .... Rangnath, confronted with such chaos, finds his text-book learning irrelevant.

'...(Shrilal Shukla writes) using vigorous, critical realism, with a rich infusion of humour and satire.'

—*The Hindustan Times*